SEPARATE JOURNEYS

SEPARATE JOURNEYS

Short Stories by
Contemporary Indian Women

Edited by
GEETA DHARMARAJAN

Introduction by Mary Ellis Gibson

of South Carolina Press

First Indian edition published by India Book Distributors, 1993
Second Indian edition published by Katha and Garutmän, 1998
American edition published in Columbia, South Carolina,
by the University of South Carolina Press, 2004

Manufactured in the United States of America

08 07 06 05 04   5 4 3 2 1

Library of Congress Cataloging-in-Publication Data

Separate journeys : short stories by contemporary Indian women / edited by Geeta
Dharmarajan ; introduction by Mary Ellis Gibson.— [1st United States ed.]
      p. cm.
   In English; translated from various Indic languages.
   Reprint. Originally published: New Delhi : Katha in association with Garutmän,
1998.
   ISBN 1-57003-551-2 (pbk. : alk. paper)
   1. Short stories, Indic—Translations into English. 2. Indic fiction—20th century—
Translations into English. 3. Indic fiction—Women authors—Translations into
English. I. Dharmarajan, Geeta. II. Gibson, Mary Ellis, 1952–
   PK5461.S37 2004
   891.4—dc22

                                                                          2004000820

Contents

INTRODUCTION

I f you were to lay a map of India over a map of the United States, it would easily cover the land from Maine to Florida, everything east of the Mississippi, plus Louisiana, Arkansas, and Missouri. Depending on how you manipulate your map, you might include a chunk of Texas as well. If you were to lay a map of the southeastern United States over a map of Europe, it would cover most of Western Europe, excluding Scandinavia. In reading European literatures from a U.S. perspective, we tend to see them in nationalist terms —German literature differing from British literature, French from Italian, etc. India, though politically unified, is at least as culturally diverse as Europe, and more marked in regional and linguistic variation; yet in reading literature from India, we again tend to subsume regional differences under a nationalist framework. The contours of this mental map were laid down in the colonial period and recast in the nationalism of the twentieth century. The mental map impacts Indian writers as well as North American readers. Most North American readers note the similarities among Indian writers or, indeed, take Indian writers of the diaspora who first publish in English in Britain and North America as representative. This collection of stories by contemporary Indian women writers defines the accomplishments of contemporary Indian fiction by almost exclusively selecting stories written in India and by representing many regions of the subcontinent.

As in the United States, in India regional differences are marked by important divergences in art, cultural life, social organization, religion, and attitudes about gender and family. As in the United States, but even more significantly, the gap between rural and urban cultures creates a second set of differences. And unlike the American literature, Indian literature—or I should say literatures—is marked by a multiplicity of languages. This anthology of stories is remarkable for representing differences of language and region and for including a variety of settings from urban, to village, to rural. The stories here —powerful evocations of women's lives and imaginations—are translated from Bangla, Kannada, Telugu, Assamese, Marathi, Hindi, Malayalam, Urdu, Tamil, and Gujarati. Two of the stories were written in English, and four have been translated by their authors.

Among recent collections of Indian short stories—those by women and those by both women and men—*Separate Journeys* is remarkable for its linguistic and regional variety. While no slender volume could possibly represent fully the diversity of women's writing in India, this collection, published jointly by StreeKatha and Garutmän in Calcutta, represents both a significant effort at collecting fine stories and an achievement in translation.

Both Garutmän and Katha—the parent of StreeKatha—are organizations formed to promote translation. Garutmän is a publishing house with a special mission to foster a community of translators of Indian languages and to provide them with assistance, with translation workshops, and with editing and distribution of translations. It co-publishes books on a nonprofit basis. Garutmän aims to "overcome the main hurdles in transcultural communication." StreeKatha is the publishing imprint of the nonprofit organization Katha, whose mission is to "spread the love of books and the joy of reading amongst children and adults, with activities spanning literacy and literature." Katha was founded with a commitment to provide high quality material for "neo-literate" children and adults in India—and to provide interactive books on women's issues in a variety of Indian languages. It also publishes magazines, pamphlets, and book series for newly literate readers, especially women and children, and provides assistance to working children and income-generating programs for poor women. *Separate Journeys* obviously owes much to Katha's dedication to improving the lives and literacy of families. Several of these stories give us a strong sense of the day-to-day lives of the poor or illiterate. This volume was one of the first published by what became Katha Vilasam, Katha's Story Research and Resource Centre, which is dedicated to fostering fiction in the regional languages of India and facilitating its translation. Katha Vilasam has grown into a vibrant organization since *Separate Journeys* was first conceived. It sponsors awards for fiction and for translation, and works with teachers and students in activities related to translation.

The complex publishing history of this anthology demonstrates clearly that English language publishing in India is often a global affair. *Separate Journeys* was originally planned in 1986 as a response to the theme of the Frankfurt Book Fair, "India: Change in Continuity." In Frankfurt, Garutmän arranged podium discussions with several authors invited from India. By 1993 the story collection was ready for publication and appeared in collaboration with India Book Distributor. The original collection had twenty-three stories. The collection was simultaneously published in London by Mantra Publishing Ltd., in an altered version. Ten of the original stories were dropped in this edition and two were added. The volume was so well received that a second Indian edition was called for. This volume appeared as a joint Katha-Garutmän publication in 1998.

The Katha-Garutmän text is the basis for this edition published by the University of South Carolina Press. In the Katha-Garutmän edition fifteen stories were included. The two stories that had been added for the Mantra edition published in London were dropped ("I Am Not Like That" by Veena Seshadri and "The Green Frock" by Charan Jit Kaur), and eight stories of the original twenty-three were also omitted ("Subhasini" by Geeta Dharmarajan; "In and Out of Parenthesis," by Saroj Pathak; "Steps," by Manjul Bhagat; "Bliss," by Abori Chhaya Devi; "The Sky and Hill," by Vasundhara Devi; "Stench of Kerosene," by Amrita Preetam; "Two Hands," by Ismat Chugtai; and "Lukose Church," by Susan Vishwanath).

This first U.S. edition, then, represents the fourth edition of *Separate Journeys,* following two Indian editions and one U.K. edition. While the words of the translated texts remain substantially the same across editions, the shifting contexts for reading are themselves significant. For most readers in the United States, these stories may well appear "Indian"; to readers in Calcutta, where they were published for Indian readers, they would appear regionally varied, distinct, and full of possible losses in translation. Obvious differences, manifest in close-up, tend to disappear with distance. This phenomenon has been described in personal terms by the writer Lakshmi Kannan, author of *India Gate and Other Stories* and *Parijata and Other Stories,* who writes in Tamil and in English, and who translates her own Tamil stories into English. In a recent interview, Kannan recounted her response to this crossing cultures: "If you go into an international setting, you realise that India is greatly respected. It is not respected for its anglicized aspect, rather it is respected for its Indianness. This is the paradox that hits you, and it amuses you when you are there, because when you come back to India there are people bending backwards to show the West that they are as good as they are. . . . The artistic lot in the international community are very drawn to Indianness. The stories that get anthologized abroad are the stories that are very ethnic." (Dhawan, 50). The "ethnicity" international readers seek is almost by definition an ethnicity constituted by generalized cultural tropes and by the international market for contemporary Indian fiction. Witness the genesis of this collection in the planning for the Frankfurt Book Fair.

International readers have come to recognize the power of such writers as Arundhati Roy, Chitra Banerjee Divakaruni, Salman Rushdie, Anita Desai, Amitav Ghosh, Meena Alexander, and Vikram Seth—wherever their work may first be published. Their fiction, like the stories collected here, may feed what Gayatri Spivak has called a "transnational U.S. multicultural hunger." "Multicultural hunger" is both a good thing—it allows one to see how large the world truly is—and a not-so-good thing. It can also create what, especially as we valorize ethnicity or gender, Spivak calls a "mask of untheorized solidarity" (xxiv, xxxvi). The stories collected here, because of their variety, may allow the North American reader to resist an easy "multiculturalism" by recognizing the complex interplay of gender, language, and culture. Geeta Dharmarajan, the editor from StreeKatha, argues that these stories allow us to understand a "self that hovers / in between / is neither man / nor woman" (xxvii). For the North American reader, an additional in-between is the cultural in-between, the place where we identify what is shared and the differences that difference makes. For Dharmarajan, each author and character, and ultimately each reader, makes a separate journey. The geography of those journeys depends very much upon one's starting place.

Separate Journeys operates for its North American readers in two registers of "multiculturalism." Its local register—as it gathers stories from across the Indian subcontinent translated from a variety of languages—may be considered analogous to regionalism in the United States. The collection and translation of stories from several languages creates a sense of regional and cultural difference. Moreover the choice of stories—particularly the attention to tribal peoples and people of scheduled castes—works toward a regional, linguistic, ethnic, and class-based representativeness much like that attempted in many anthologies of women's writing from North America. Like these anthologies, *Separate Journeys* addresses communalism (sectarian/religious differences) and social injustice in its own national context by crossing divides of language, religion, gender, and social class. The anthology begins with Mahasweta Devi's story "Bayen," about a low-caste woman, whose caste-assigned job is to bury children who are not old enough for cremation. Chandi is declared a bayen, or witch, when, after she is blamed unjustly for the death of her niece, she is no longer able to bury children and guard the burial ground. She begins to hallucinate, pressed by the intolerable burden of her inherited, culturally assigned job and what would appear to be postpartum depression. The villagers, including her drunken husband, respond by declaring her a bayen and casting her out. Devi's story, translated from the Bangla, is kin to those by Mamoni Raisom Goswami and Kamala Das in its empathy with and representation of combined class/caste and gendered differences. Mamoni Raisom Goswami's story, "The Empty Chest," translated from the Assamese, brings us again to the degradation associated in India with handling the dead: Toradoi has served in the house of the zamindar, or land/estate owner, and has "given herself" to his son who, forbidden to marry her, dies years later in an accident. By this time Toradoi's husband is jailed for a drunken accident and her sons go hungry. She scavenges from the cremation ground the chest that contained her former lover's body in a futile attempt to undo the damage that is her life. Kamala Das's story, "The Hijra," translated from the Malayalam, centers on a Gujarati woman who has lost her transgendered daughter. The daughter, the story implies, was sold by her paternal grandmother and her father to the hijras (transvestites, eunuchs, and transgendered people who act as prostitutes and, in rituals, confer fertility and prosperity on houses to which male children are born). Seeking the girl years later, her mother cannot recognize her, despite her beauty and her birthmark, for the girl, now grown, lives a foreign—and in its way disreputable—life. The old woman, guided by blue lights of the railway station, returns toward her home, at the ominous English address—Warden Road. These three stories along with others in the collection create a broad frame of reference for North American readers. Regional, class, caste, and gendered differences, especially in contrast to stories of middle-class life, resist homogenization of the "other culture."

A second register in which this collection operates is the register of international "multiculturalism"—those necessarily simplified notions of national identity or ethnicity Kannan and Spivak identify. Yet the regional, cultural, class, and ethnic differences represented in this anthology also give North American readers ample opportunity to resist simplification. A story like "The Hijra" resonates by raising the question of how cultures "place" those who do not fit dualistic definitions of sex and gender.

Found in Translation

Despite the variety of stories and original languages represented in *Separate Journeys,* monolingual Americans may still not be able easily to recognize what is lost in translation. In her edited collection of stories by Indian women, Lakshmi Holmström points to the potential loss of nuance in translation—citing, for example, the way the terseness of Tamil grammatical structure is difficult to render in English, or the way English lacks single words to differentiate between a mother's sister and a mother's brother's wife. Such differences may have the effect for international readers of flattening the nuances of geography or of domestic space (Holmström, xvi).

The choice to publish these stories in English appears a matter of course to us in North America. For English speakers in North America, "translation" simply means translation into English. In India the choice of English is logical but more complex, more ideologically fraught. The issues of translation have been put most succinctly by Susie Tharu and K. Lalita in their introduction to *Women Writing in India* (published in two volumes by the Feminist Press in 1993) They characterize translation as a collision of worlds, often unequal worlds at that. In their own anthology of texts from eleven languages and as many centuries, they acknowledge: "We have been very aware that in India, when we translate a regional language—Tamil or Oriya, for instance—into English, we are representing a regional culture for a more powerful national or 'Indian' one, and when this translation is made available to a readership outside India, we are also representing a national culture for a still more powerful international culture—which is today, in effect, a Western one" (2:xx).

Geeta Dharmarajan, the editor of *Separate Journeys*, embarked on a quest similar to Tharu and Lalita's, seeking stories in many languages. She says in her introduction to this volume that when she assembled the translations, she "understood all over again how difficult it is to clump all literature produced in India or by Indians under the umbrella statement 'Indian.' The term itself is so deliciously vague and comprises so many regions, so many varied cultures, so many styles and traditions of writing. The tradition that a writer in Urdu instinctively knows and adopts is most probably unknown to her counterpart in Karnataka who weaves her story in Kannada" (xxviii). Despite its difficulties, the need for translation is urgent, for, as Dharmarajan notes, the speaker of Urdu may well be unable to read Kannada and vice versa. Even as English provides global readers access to these stories, so too it serves as an important link language among readers in India.

Whatever power differentials may be operating, normally we think of translation as occurring between a source and a target language, with the target language being the vernacular of the intended readers. English in India is more complex. Linguists often make a further distinction between vernacular and vehicular languages—the vernacular being the spoken language, the vehicular used for communication among speakers of different vernaculars, as nineteenth-century French or medieval Latin was used for diplomatic purposes. Indian English has a shifting status as both a vernacular and a vehicular language. As one of three languages in which pan-Indian literature is written, or into which it is translated—the others being Hindi and Sanskrit—English serves as a vehicular language, a means of moving information, creative materials, etc., between languages (Kachru, 69). For some Indian writers, however, English is not a vehicular language but one, sometimes one of several, mother tongues.

Responding to the social complexities of Indian English, editors of Indian fiction in recent years have taken various approaches to the issue of translation. The most inflammatory position is certainly the simplest—choose English. Remind your readers that for some Indian writers, both in India and in the diaspora, English is a mother or at least another mother tongue. The strongest version of this position is surely Salman Rushdie's claim in introducing the anthology *Mirrorwork: Fifty Years of Indian Writing, 1947–1997* (1997), that "prose writing—both fiction and non-fiction—created in this period by Indian writers *working in English* is proving to be a stronger and more important body of work than most of what has been produced in the 16 'official languages' of India, the so-called 'vernacular languages,' during the same time; and, indeed, this new and still burgeoning, 'Indo-Anglian' literature represents perhaps the most valuable contribution India has yet made to the world of books" (viii). Obviously this statement has been inflammatory enough to draw down yet another controversy upon Rushdie's oft controversial head. While Rushdie and Elizabeth West's anthology does make for some very fine reading, collections such as *Separate Journeys* or Susie Tharu and K. Lalita's *Women Writing in India* make clear Rushdie's assessment leaves something to be desired and much unsaid. Rushdie evaluates the contemporary canon but does not attempt to speak for the archival recovery work represented in Tharu and Lalita's volumes.

Sweeping judgments of literary merit have the virtue of being impossible to prove or disprove. Rushdie's judgment, though, does reveal one kind of position, that of the writer who is born and/or educated to English in India and abroad. Perhaps we could characterize the "language position" of a writer (or a translator) in the same way feminist critics characterize her or his "subject position"; from this perspective a language position would be a social location partially defined by language as it intersects with class, education, gender, region, and the constitution of national subjects. For some writers in India or the diaspora—like Rushdie—English serves as a vernacular. For others, it is a mother other tongue—not spoken at home most of the time but occasionally —and read and spoken at school. For still others it is an acquisition of a second and not-quite-foreign language, still further removed from a language or languages spoken at home. Moreover, whatever a writer's languages, the judgments made about language, translation, and the status of English are intimately tied to positions about nation. In surveying postcolonial critics' positions on issues of translation, Douglas Robinson marks a distinction between postcolonial theorists who "celebrate hybridity" and thus view translation in a "utopian light, as a channel of resistance and self-preservation," and those "drawn to a vision of precolonial paradise and the evils of empire," who are more likely to "demonize" translation (95).

The editors of *Separate Journeys* and other collections of writing by Indian women inhabit a middle ground. A feminist approach to Indian culture before independence is unlikely to result in a "vision of a precolonial paradise," and for women in postcolonial India "hybridity" figures more often as a narrative of displacement than as a utopian condition. For, as in the discourses of race and gender in the United States, women in India are complexly situated in the discourses of nationalism and gender. Tharu and Lalita argue that the processes of Indian nationalism resulted in another kind of translation—the translation of "heterogeneous articulations" of cultural forms into a new form of authority, essentially "upper-caste, middle-class, and male point of view of the agent-state" (57). In this new articulation and in traditional culture, women, and particularly feminists, are always already other. Translation from various vernaculars into English, in consequence, is seen in a nuanced way—as neither intrinsically positive nor intrinsically a capitulation to Western authority. Rather, translation may serve to create what Spivak would call a theorized solidarity among women.

Separate Journeys, unlike *Mirrorwork,* represents the work of writers in the vernacular languages of India and those, like Kamala Das, who write or translate in more than one language. For many of these writers, the "language position" is complex—dependent on schooling, home, region, and the subtle processes of thought and imagination created by these factors. A vivid account of the kind of linguistic complexity taken for granted by Indian writers, including many in this collection, is provided by Shashi Deshpande, one of the best known women writers in India. Replying to questions about her decision to write in English, Deshpande gives the following account of her childhood: "Ours was by no means a Westernized household. Apart from the fact that we lived in a small town, in a middle class family, there was the fact that my father taught Sanskrit in college, he wrote in Kannada, read English and had married a Marathi wife. Home was a harmonious mix of languages. Kalidas and Bhavabhuti, Shivaram Karanth and Masti Venkatesh Iyengar were names as familiar as Ibsen and Shaw. And if in school we did Wordsworth and Tennyson, at home we had to learn the *Amarkosha* by heart. Nevertheless, all reading was in English." Deshpande goes on to describe her regret at feeling cut off "from my own language and literature." Though she taught herself to read Kannada and Marathi, nonetheless "English was and remained the language of my thinking, it was and is the language in which I expressed myself" (Jain, 30–31). Deshpande acknowledges that readers often ask why she writes in English and that, whatever her answer, the exchange is always ideologically fraught. English is both her own language—"the language of my thinking"—and understood as paradoxically not her own. She does not claim the same relationship to English that she believes her father had to Kannada or her mother to Marathi.

The paradox then for Indian readers, writers, and translators, lies precisely in the "owning" of English as a language for writing or translation. Rushdie claims outright ownership and the right to experimentation that goes with it. For Deshpande and others ownership is more difficult but still crucial. As the linguist Braj Kachru argues, "using a non-native language in native context to portray new themes, characters, and situations is like redefining the semantic and semiotic potential of a language, making language mean something which is not part of its traditional 'meaning.' It is an attempt to give a new African or Asian identity, and thus an extra dimension of meaning. A part of that dimension perhaps remains obscure or mysterious to the Western reader" (317). This process of creating new meanings in English, for those who write in two languages or translate their own work, like Mrinal Pande, Kamala Das, Qurratulain Hyder, and Varsha Das in this volume, is a process of transcreation

(Kachru, 319). The creation of new meanings accompanies the creation of new identities.

Those of us who cannot read these stories in the original languages can see only some of the decisions translators have made, word by word, to make these stories available to Indian and then to global audiences. As the editor, Geeta Dharmarajan, puts it, these stories are woven into "something that looks whole to the outsider who does not see the warp and woof" (xxviii). Perhaps the warp and woof of Indian cultures and languages are most visible in a text like Mrinal Pande's "A Kind of Love Story." Here Pande has translated her own story from Hindi, making judicious choices about which words to translate, which few to leave transliterated, and which to explain. Pande's main character, Madhusudan Babu, spends his life avoiding life, having learned from his teacher of classical Indian music—a man with three wives—to avoid the company of women. Pande's story turns on delicate, though searing, irony as Madhusudan, now an old misanthrope, falls in a kind of love. Madhusudan's teacher, he believes, experienced music as a *siddhi*, a spiritual accomplishment, which he should have passed on in some measure to his student. The gift is wasted, if indeed it ever existed at all, and when Madhusudan has the opportunity to share it and the lives of others, he resorts to lies to win affection. So much for music as *siddhi*. Madhusudan ends in his local temple, ironically, "listening to holy chants." Pande's delicate choices in translation allow her English-speaking readers both at home and abroad to experience the ironies at this intersection of traditional culture, art, and misogyny. The languages of classical music and religion move into English only partially, most often transliterated rather than explained; the vocabulary of music retains its specificity. In the process we see the distance between musical skill and the spirit of religious music, between *siddhi* as discipline and personal rigidity.

Pande takes "the reader to the author" or to the author's culture, asking us to appreciate musical intricacies; Anita Desai "takes the author to the reader," that is, she gives the monolingual English reader a great deal of information (Robinson, 1). In one of the two stories in *Separate Journeys* that were originally written in English, Desai's "Private Tuition with Mr. Bose," the teaching of literature is of central concern. Yet Desai's story represents body language as the most eloquent communication of all. (For American readers, it is useful to know that "tuition" in Indian English means lessons or tutoring, not school fees.) On his balcony in Calcutta Mr. Bose tutors reluctant teenagers in Sanskrit and Bangla poetry. The boy who, supposedly, studies Sanskrit is surly; the girl tortures him. In response to his discomfiture, Mr. Bose's wife speaks with her hands, rattling pots and pans, making purees in the kitchen. Desai captures the ridiculous: "He had quite forgotten that his next pupil, this Wednesday, was to be Upneet . . . this once-a-week typhoon, Upneet of the floral sari, ruby

earrings and shaming laughter. Under this Upneet's gaze such ordinary functions of a tutor's life as sitting down at a table, sharpening a pencil . . . became
matters of farce, disaster and hilarity. . . . Throwing away the Sanskrit books,
bringing out volumes of Bangla poetry, opening to a poem by Jibanandan Das,
he wondered ferociously: Why did she come? What use had she for Bangla
poetry? Why did she come from that house across the road where the loud
radio rollicked, to sit on his balcony, in view of his shy wife, making him read
poetry to her? It was intolerable. Intolerable, all of it—except, only for the
seventy-five rupees paid at the end of the month. Oranges, he thought grimly,
and milk, medicines, clothes. And he read to her." For the next half hour
Upneet tortures her tutor, swinging her foot in rhythm, lifting the hem of her
sari as he reads to her the Bangla poetry he had once copied out for his wife.
The "two halves of the difficult world that he had been holding so carefully
together, sealing them with reams of poetry, reams of Sanskrit" split apart
"into dissonance." Desai's English captures the rhythms of poetry (which she
translates) and the rhythms of the silence between Mr. Bose and Upneet, Mr.
Bose and his nameless wife. By narrating small actions and bodily dispositions
Desai conveys the wife's irritation and the couple's silent affection. Finally the
"grammar" between wife and husband rearranges itself. Desai's English rhythms
match the rhythms of domestic activity. Mr. Bose's multiple languages are less
important than the rhythms of the body and the wordless language and even
the small talk of daily life.

Both of these stories examine the intersections of traditional high culture
and gender; in both stories, traditional arts only seem to hold together the
worlds of domesticity and learning. In these as in other stories in this volume,
the grammar of tradition alone does not make for happiness. Translation operates in the messy present, not in an imagined precolonial paradise or a puta-
tive hybrid utopia. Dissonance, as William Carlos Williams famously said,
leads to discovery.

Women Writers
Gender and Nation

The stories in *Separate Journeys* represent different languages, posing literal
problems of translation. They also represent the problematics of translation in
a more figurative way—as gender and sexuality are made to stand in for, to
represent, or to translate new political and economic realities. Historians of
Indian women's writing in the twentieth century connect it to the history of
Indian feminism, tracing the relationship between women's movements in
India to other political movements, especially nationalism, and to innovations
in literary theme and form. While a recapitulation of this history is beyond the
scope of an introduction like this one, I want to suggest briefly how the stories

in *Separate Journeys* do represent these larger cultural trends. In their monograph-length introduction to the two volumes of *Women Writing in India*, Susie Tharu and K. Lalita outline the importance for twentieth-century women writers of the high nationalism of the Swadeshi movement, the liberalism of national women's organizations that developed out of earlier reform movements focused on women's education and social and legal position, and the socialist commitments of women involved in the Progressive Writers' Association in the first half of the twentieth century.

The Swadeshi movement, valorizing what was of "of one's own country" as opposed to goods imported literally or intellectually from the colonial ruler and other Western powers, created new meanings of everyday life, reformulating nationalism in terms of "authentic Indianness," and making gender crucial to this Indianness (Tharu and Lalita, 73). Tharu and Lalita identify the figure of the traditional Hindu upper-caste and middle-class grandmother as the embodiment of tradition, one who remakes, contains, and continues tradition however "secular" it may look through the century. Not surprisingly *Separate Journeys* begins with just such a figure. Geeta Dharmarajan begins with a tale of her own storytelling grandmother who fed her fascinated grandchildren snacks of rice and sambar as they listened to her stories.

In addition to the definitions of gender and nation constituted through the Swadeshi movement, national women's organizations also contributed to fiction writing by women in numerous ways—through political activity, as well as agitation around issues that had been debated since the nineteenth century, including most notably, education, dowry, child marriage, purdah, and the prohibition of widow remarriage (Tharu and Lalita, 84). Lakshmi Holmström and other critics have shown how these issues formed both fiction and autobiography in the last century-and-a-half. Holmström cites as precedents for work emerging from twentieth-century women's organizations such texts from the nineteenth century as Ramabai Saraswati's *The High-Caste Hindu Woman* and Krupabai Satthianadhan's *Saguna*. "New-Woman" writing from the turn of the century, like Krupabai's two books, began a tradition carried on in the 1910s and 1920s (Forbes, Lokugé), when in concert with nationalist struggles the emphasis shifted from social reforms to the franchise (Tharu and Lalita, 85). By the 1930s in the nationalist struggle, women's issues were often subsumed under the terms of liberal nationalism, in much the same way, ironically, that women's insistence on the franchise took a backseat to male working-class struggles for political and economic power in nineteenth-century Britain (for details of liberal nationalism, see Forbes and Tharu and Lalita, 88).

A different strain of feminism and writing by women in the years before and during the Second World War was associated with the more radical socialist program of the Progressive Writers' Associations, which formed all over the country. Of the writers represented in *Separate Journeys* both Mahasweta Devi and Anupama Niranjana were active in the PWAs. The PWAs opposed both fascism and imperialism. Out of this movement also came an active theater movement that was significant for many women writers, a commitment still important for Mahasweta Devi. In the immediate postwar years the PWA lost much of its strength.

A second wave of the twentieth-century women's movement, however, helped shape writing by women in the 1970s. The Emergency, 1975–77, with its curtailment of freedoms and other repressive measures, catalyzed various forms of resistance. Women became radicalized, working in trade unions, cooperatives, organizations of slum dwellers and tribal peoples (Holmström). As in the reformist women's movements of the nineteenth and twentieth centuries, in the new movements of the 1970s and since, representation of poverty and of tribal peoples could be a radical force for social change, or it could consolidate ideology around an image of rural India presented from a middle-class perspective. Just as the Swadeshi movement and reformist tendencies in the women's movement allowed women to be assimilated to a traditionalist (and implicitly Hindu) ideology, so too could work arising from the second wave of twentieth-century feminism in India. Urmila Pawar's story, translated here from the Marathi, perhaps comes closest to this kind of ideological representation of rural India. Pawar's story, "Justice," however manages to skirt the temptations of representing the rural simplistically from a middle-class point of view by ironizing the prejudices of the city-dwelling narrator. The heroine of the story (of course named Parvati, daughter of the Himalaya, perfect consort, and a form of the mother goddess Devi) defends motherhood, assumes she bears a son, and speaks up for herself in a way that would seem to personify rural Indian virtues. The narration could also be said to be yet another treatment of the plight of the young widow. But Urmila Pawar frames the story through the middle-class consciousness of the male city-dwelling narrator, who comes to grips with his own past. The narrator's contempt for the countryside and his natal village could be translated on an ideological register into contempt for India—but also contempt for the lower classes. Parvati's courage and forthrightness teach him a lesson. The ironic reverberations of the story's ending allow the complexities of rural/urban, upper-/lower-class relationships to surface and to create dissonance, though such ironies never call into question Parvati's paradigmatic status.

Ashapurna Devi's story "Izzat" similarly uses a narrative framing device that allows the author to foreground the problems of the middle class by representing the experiences of working-class women. In Devi's story Basanti, a maidservant, pleads with her old mistress to protect the honor of her daughter, who is being harassed by rough men in her neighborhood. Sumitra, the mistress, finally agrees, only to realize that her husband forbids it. The beautiful but poor daughter becomes sexual prey, but Sumitra finds herself powerless to protect her. Set in Calcutta, the story turns on the middle-class dilemma of Sumitra and, without overtly minimizing Basanti's suffering, draws parallels between her helplessness and Sumitra's own. Basanti assures Sumitra that in her comfortable home she is "queen," but Sumitra soon learns that her power is only nominal. Without Basanti's daughter's anger, the story would rest wholly within the problematics of middle-class life. The girl—a teenager who says what she thinks—makes her own clear-eyed judgments about patronizing the poor, but the story focuses on Sumitra's potential awakening to the limitations of her own position. One is reminded of southern U.S. stories of white middle-class characters awakening to the realities of racism—racism understood from what the white characters perceive to be the "center."

Recent stories about tribal people and stories that create glimpses of a utopian vision through fantasy or a kind of magical realism resist both the submerged communalism implied in the figure of the Hindu grandmother and liberal narratives of nationalism as well. Among the most powerful stories in this collection, Devi's "Bayen" evokes a community apart from, and yet obliquely dependent on, the wider world, a community where children are not vaccinated and tradition holds little protection for any woman who steps out of her assigned place, however intolerable it might be. Chandidasi, the servant of the burial ground, experiences the weight of tradition in her body, her mother's milk. Cast out and turned into a pariah, driven mad by isolation, she dies in an almost surreal attempt to prevent a train wreck. Swallowed in the train's light, Chandi dies to become, ironically, a hero in death. Distances of caste and gender, rural and urban are never bridged.

Other stories in this volume embrace experimental approaches to psyche and culture. "I," by Jeelani Bano, explores the fractured inner world of a boy who, for reasons unclear, cannot believe himself to be the child of his own mother. The mother-son dyad is repeatedly ruptured as the son takes literally every figurative pronouncement, every remark like "this crying child cannot be mine." Amir, who seems to be a favored son of a relatively fortunate family, cannot overcome the psychological place of the orphan. Again, trains figure as emblems of modernity. The train marks Amir's sense of division from self and family. Interestingly, it is the son, who need not necessarily leave home, rather than a daughter, who experiences loss of self and family. Modernity itself is equated with the boy's inability to recognize his mother, his sisters, or his own identity.

The Art of Story
Feminist Recasting of Oral and Poetic Traditions

The great majority of stories here represent the dominant tradition in twentieth-century Indian as well as in English fiction: realism. The well-crafted tale turns usually on a single incident and implies a wider network of social and psychological relationships. "Bayen" and "I" push the edges of these conventions, the first drawing on elements of folk tradition and the second on modernist stream of consciousness. Other stories in the collection, notably "The Sermons of Haji Gul Baba Bektashi" owe much to very different oral traditions. Almost a Sufi tall tale, Qurratulain Hyder's work reminds us that Urdu traditions are also among the rich sources of story in Indian culture. Oral tradition and poetry form the context for other stories as well.

The final story in the collection is something of a prose poem and perhaps also a political allegory. Varsha Das's story, translated by the author under the title "I Am Complete," is the most direct treatment of women's sensual experience in a collection that is relatively reticent on the topic. The speaker of the story is freed, from what we do not know—prison, marriage? She remembers a now lost lover but is rescued from longing as the sky showers its own affection on her, caressing her, admonishing her that such a love would have turned to hatred. Achieving freedom through the earth's motherly intervention, the speaker becomes serene: "If I open my arms I can embrace the whole universe. I am complete."

A similar, but less optimistic representation of wholeness comes in "The Widows of Tithoor." Perhaps the most complexly experimental story in *Separate Journeys*, it is also the only one to deal directly with India before independence. Viswapria L. Iyengar's work creates a glimpse of an imagined resistance to both patriarchal and imperialist structures of power. "The Widows of Tithoor" is among the most haunting in the collection, and indeed it is about haunting. We discover that the Collector, a colonial official—one of the White Ghosts—seems to be responsible for the death of a local widow, who, like the bayen, is so marginalized as to be thought a witch. He has declared the widow Haldi a subversive because she has created her own religious ritual for local widows—found her own solution to the "problem" of the Hindu widow as the British conceived it. And she is suspect too because she has been seen with "Veerappa, the rebel leader from Pithoor." By shaping point of view and creating an elaborate interweaving of narrative times, Viswapria Iyengar makes Haldi a legend and creator of legends, something between a priest and a goddess. Under Haldi's direction, the widows' newfound freedom, value, sensual life, and community form a utopian moment of resistance within repressive regimes of power. In the end, Haldi's religious community has no temple, no text, only the scraps of a legend that even the participants in the ritual can almost come to doubt. Haldi herself, it is implied, is burned to death. "The widows of Tithoor never ventured to inquire into her disappearance. In their silence, and her songs, some of the story remained. . . . The jackfruit trees shed their heavy rocklike fruit on the jagged peaks, sweet-pungent fragrance enveloped the hill for many days."

What remains of Haldi is the memory of resistance incorporated in scraps of legend and poetry. In portraying Haldi's spiritual power, Iyengar draws on the traditional imagery of *bhakti* (devotional) poetry of the eighth through the sixteenth centuries. The various bhakti movements were strongly linked to the artisan classes, and, at least in their earlier stages, were more open to women than many other poetic traditions. In the scraps of Haldi's poem, the woman poet's spiritual devotion to the male god is replaced by the goddess, but the sensual power of the poetry remains. Haldi's initiation ballad reads:

> Wild jasmines, weave the wind with the stars.
> Crown my flowing hair.
> Sun, smudge your evening blood on my forehead.
> Mother Moon, I will swim
> With your silver scales in the river.
> I will eat crystal sugar and drink date wine. For
> tonight I am bride unto myself.

Haldi symbolically marries herself; the widowed initiate does the same. Earth itself becomes the spouse. Haldi's ballad transforms the bhakta women poets' devotion to the god into a female-defined tradition. Within the separate community of women it revives the erotic power of its predecessors. Compare with Haldi's ballad, for example, these lines from Akkamahadevi, a twelfth-century Virasaiva poet who wrote in Kannada:

> It was like a stream
> running into the dry bed
> of a lake,
>
>   like rain
> pouring on plants
> parched to sticks.
>
> It was like this world's pleasure
> and the way to the other,
>   both
> walking towards me.

Seeing the feet of the master,
O lord white as jasmine,
I was made
worthwhile.
(Ramanujan, Speaking of Siva, *118)*

In this beautiful translation, A. K. Ramanujan captures the poet's search for this world's pleasure and the way to another, for the balance she achieves in the final lines, "I was made / worthwhile." Iyengar's imagined ritual transforms this sense of completion to self-completion: "I am bride unto myself."

The writers in *Separate Journeys* take the quest for wholeness into the worlds of middle-class domesticity, poverty, violence, and colonial history. They work through various languages and literary traditions. They embrace divergent literary conventions, ranging from realism to didactic fiction to stream of consciousness and experimental tales. They reach out to worlds both local and global. It will be exciting to see in the twenty-first century what worlds walk back toward them.

MARY ELLIS GIBSON

Works Cited

Alexander, Meena. *Illiterate Heart.* Evanston, Ill.: TriQuarterly Books, 2002.

Desai, Anita. *Baumgartner's Bombay.* New York: Penguin, 1989.

————. *Diamond Dust and Other Stories.* London: Vintage, 2001.

Deshpande, Shasi. "Of Concerns, Of Anxieties." In *Women in Indo-Anglian Fiction: Tradition and Modernity*, edited by Narish K. Jain, 28–37. Shimla: Indian Institute of Advanced Study, Manohar, 1998.

Dhawan, R. K., ed. *Indian Women Writers.* New Delhi: Prestige, 2001.

Divakaruni, Chitra. *The Mistress of Spices.* New York: Anchor Books, 1997.

————. *The Unknown Errors of Our Lives.* New York: Doubleday, 2001.

Forbes, Geraldine Hancock. *Women in Modern India.* Cambridge: Cambridge University Press, 1996.

Ghosh, Amitav. *The Glass Palace.* New York: Random House, 2001.

————. *In an Antique Land.* New York: Vintage Books, 1994.

Holmström, Lakshmi, ed. *The Inner Courtyard: Stories by Indian Women.* London: Virago Press, 1990.

Jain, Narish K. *Women in Indo-Anglian Fiction: Tradition and Modernity.* Shimla: Indian Institute of Advanced Study, Manohar, 1998.

Kachru, Braj B. "Models for Non-Native Englishes." In *The Other Tongue: English across Cultures*, 2d ed., edited by Braj B. Kachru, 48–74. Delhi: Oxford University Press, 1996.

Kannan, Lakshmi. *India Gate and Other Stories.* New Delhi: Orient, Longman, 1993.

———. "Ranjana Harish in Conversation with Lakshmi Kannan." In *Indian Women Writers,* edited by R. K. Dhawan. New Delhi: Prestige, 2001.

Lokugé, Chandani. "Cross-Cultural Transformations and a Pioneer Indian-English Woman Writer." In *From Commonwealth to Post-Colonial*, edited by Anna Rutherford, 102–16. Aarhus: Dangaroo, 1992.

Ramanujan, A. K. *Speaking of Siva.* Baltimore: Penguin, 1973.

Robinson, Douglas. *Translation and Empire: Postcolonial Theories Explained.* Manchester: St. Jerome Publishing, 1997.

Roy, Arundhati. *The Cost of Living.* New York: Modern Library, 1999.

——— *The God of Small Things.* New York: Random House, 1997.

Rushdie, Salman, and Elizabeth West, eds. *Mirrorwork: Fifty Years of Indian Writing, 1947–1997.* New York: Henry Holt, 1997.

Saraswati, Ramabai. *The High-Caste Hindu Woman.* 1888. Reprint, New Delhi: Inter India Publications, 1984.

Satthianadhan, Krupabai. *Saguna: The First Autobiographical Novel in English by an Indian Woman.* Edited by Chandani Lokugé. Delhi: Oxford University Press, 1998.

Seth, Vikram. *An Equal Music.* New York: Broadway Books, 1999.

———. *A Suitable Boy.* New York: Harper Collins, 1993.

Spivak, Gayatri, ed. and trans. *Mahasveta Debi: Imaginary Maps.* New York: Routledge, 1995.

Tharu, Susie, and K. Lalita, eds. *Women Writing in India.* 2 vols. New York: The Feminist Press, 1993.

Additional Short Story Collections and Critical Works

Amireh, Amal, and Lisa Suhair Majaj. *Going Global: The Transnational Reception of Third World Women Writers.* New York: Garland, 2000.

Bai, Meera. *Women's Voices: The Novels of Indian Women Writers.* New Delhi: Prestige, 1996.

Behl, Aditya, and David Nicholls, eds. *The Penguin New Writing in India.* New York: Penguin Books, 1995.

Burton, Antoinette. *Burdens of History: British Feminists, Indian Women, and Imperial Culture, 1865–1915.* Chapel Hill: University of North Carolina Press, 1994.

Butalea, Urvashi, and Rita Menon, eds. *In Other Words: New Writing by Indian Women.* New Delhi: Kali for Women, 1992.

Chatterjee, Chandra. *The World Within: A Study of Novels in English by Indian Women.* New Delhi: Radha Publications, 1996.

Chaudhuri, Amit. *Picador Book of Modern Indian Literature.* London: Picador, 2001.

Kali for Women, eds. *Truth Tales: Contemporary Stories by Women Writers of India.* New York: Feminist Press, 1990.

Kohli, Suresh, ed. *Savvy: Stories by Indian Women Writers*. New Delhi: Arnold Publishers, 1992.

Lal, Malashri. *The Law of the Threshold: Women Writers in Indian English*. Shimla: Indian Institute of Advanced Study, 1995.

Mathur, Divya. *Odyssey: Short Stories by Indian Women Writers Settled Abroad*. London: Asian Book Shop, 1998.

Mukherjee, Meenakshi. *The Perishable Empire: Essays on Indian Writing in English*. New York: Oxford University Press, 2000.

Mukundan, Monisha, ed. *Mosaic: New Writings from Award-Winning British and Indian Writers*. New York: Penguin Books, 1998.

Prasad, Madhusudan, ed. *Contemporary Indian-English Stories*. New Delhi: Sterling Publishers, 1984.

Roy, Anuradha. *Patterns of Feminist Consciousness in Indian Women Writers*. New Delhi: Prestige Books, 1999.

Seshadri, Vijayalakshmi. *The New Woman in Indian English: Women Writers since the 1970s*. Delhi: B. R. Publishing, 1995.

Singh, Avadesh Kumar. *Indian Feminisms*. New Delhi: Creative Books, 2001.

Wasi, Jehanara, ed. *Storehouse of Tales: Contemporary Indian Women Writers*. New Delhi: Srishti Publishers, 2001.

INTRODUCTION TO THE
FIRST INDIAN EDITION

I grew up in South India in the early sixties. I remember long evenings spent on the tall front steps to my grandmother's home, listening to her stories, while we ate the neat little round balls of rice and sambar and vegetable or papad that she placed in our palms. We were seven, no, eight of us, sisters and aunts and uncles. And we all ate and listened, listened and ate, both at the same time, because when our turn came we had to be ready with an empty palm or forego our share till the next round. And then, as if to add to the magic, sometimes there would be all-night harikathas, told by well known story tellers, usually men. Massive bronze oil lamps burned on the stage, under the pandals, as old stories took on new dimensions, transformed themselves into fresh fantasies, as if the great epics were being minted again, sparked off by a new creativity. And when it was over I remember walking home, through silent streets that echoed the stories told and retold in a myriad of laughing, admiring voices. None of these stories veered even an iota from what we had heard.

Thousands of years ago the Rig Veda spoke of women as worthy beings walking in the shade of the mother goddess, the creator of all things, though even here we see some ambivalence which was to harden and turn itself into the rigid codes of conduct that still hold Indian women captive, in life as well as in literature. In post-Vedic India, prayers were for sons and grandsons; never for girls. Forgiveness, too. And literacy. The wisdom of the sages was not for women. Nothing much has changed in the two thousand years since—for most women. Stifled to such a degree that they could not even see themselves as being suppressed, where was the question of writing to express oneself, or, if one did, of seeing beyond the stated and the known?

When I was growing up, I knew of only one woman who did not merely get married and have children. She wrote stories. Her stories were published And some of her friends didn't know what to do with her. Had she been a classical dancer for instance (as a few were), they would have known how to react. At least a dancer did not express forbidden and secret feelings, only emoted to words written by others about the love of the human soul for the immortal, about the atma and the paramatma. A woman writer had to think about being "decent" in ways the dancer didn't have to, for dance forms have their own acceptable parameters—the lovelorn lover, the faithful wife, the good mother. To get out of this web that closes in from all sides, a woman needs extraordinary strength and self-confidence. This is what the women Bhakta poets who wrote more than a thousand years ago had plenty of. Like the dancer, they too created within the apparently narrow parameters of religion but, reading them now, I am wonder-struck at the space they won for themselves within those confines. Avvai, Bahinabai, Mira Bai, Mahadeviakka, Karaik-kalammai, Lalla Ded, Chandravati—to name a few—counseled kings and talked of stagecraft. They spoke their minds, many looked far beyond the limits laid by femininity, even the individuality of the sexes.

Sings Dasimayya:

> If they see
> breasts and long hair coming
> they call it woman,
>
> if beard and whiskers
> they call it man:
>
> but, look, the self that hovers
> in between
> is neither man
> nor woman
>
> O Ramanatha
> (trans. A. K. Ramanujan,
> Speaking of Siva, 1973)

If some contemporary women writers have been able to slough off the inhibitions and restrictions laid down by age-old codes, it is the extraordinary women poets of the tenth century who must be seen as their role models.

To go down history quickly, till the mid–nineteenth century, not only were writers predominantly male, the readers were also invariably so. Literacy amongst women was abominably low. It was only after women in well-to-do homes started having tutors at home that we find Indian women writing again. In Tamil, for instance, we have the rather bold novel by Devakunjari Ammal, *Vijayalakshmi* (1906). And in Gujarati, around the same time, there were a handful of women who used the medium of the short story to protest about the way women were being treated. By the 1930s, short stories were appearing in almost all the Indian languages, with writers like Rabindranath Tagore getting serious about it. And we find women writers becoming more visible, though they still had to walk in the shadow of their male contemporaries. As they do even now.

"Decency" still plagues the woman writer. Some of them do use the medium of fantasy to explore sensitive areas. But not everyone is gutsy, or able to write fantasies; and it is common to hear the accusation that women writers tend to stick to "safe, decent" ideas. Reading *Separate Journeys,* one may not always agree with this criticism. The writers represented here prove that Indian women no longer need the all-enveloping garb of religion, or the stealth of subversion to say what they want. The women writers of India seem to have come into their own once and for all. Finally.

This collection explores the human predicament and we find that the grammar has a way of not always arranging itself "according to rule" as the protagonist in Anita Desai's story discovers. Each separate journey in this book takes us places we have been to, each of us in our own unexplored ways. Whether it is Ramakrishnaiah ("The Decision"), the old reserved teacher who is shaken out of a placid existence by the entry of a pregnant woman, or Madhusudan Babu ("A Kind of Love Story") who resorts to the only way he can think of to get something he wants, or Paru in "Justice," a woman who talks back to a whole panchayat, we find the stories urge us to cross the minuscule chasm between all that is male and female. Male and female characteristics merge and blend and we find that we are looking at ". . . the self that hovers / in between / [that] is neither man / nor woman." A realization of self finally, is what journeys are or should be all about. And for our women to reach where Dasimayya was a thousand years ago has taken a lot of individual courage and hard work.

Talking of journeys takes my mind back to journeys I have made, with a little twig of green neem tucked into my sari, a small prayer revolving in the mind, a certain excitement about the destination. Every journey has its departure, naturally, and its arrival. And in the journeys that each writer, each character makes in these stories, the departures and arrivals are significant, if not always pronounced. Each journey though also means transformations, and transformations of whatever kind are what most stories are made of. Transformations were a speciality of Indian myths; stories that gave form and image to a whole range of human experiences, thus allowing them to travel from the private realm of the dreamer into public domain. Metaphors and similes have been used by ancient Indians to view their world and make sense out of it and, in these stories, we find the writers resorting often to the tricks that they learned while sitting on their grandmothers' laps maybe, hearing stories while they had their night meals under a sky of moon and stars.

When I was working on this collection, I found the most exciting aspect of India proved to be the most frustrating also: her many languages. How does one even start when stories are being written in all of the twenty-two officially-recognized languages of India, not to mention the dialects, that could take the list up to nearly seven hundred! I understood all over again how difficult it is to clump all literature produced in India or by Indians under the umbrella statement "Indian." The term itself is so deliciously vague and comprises so many regions, so many varied cultures, so many styles and traditions of writing. The tradition that a writer in Urdu instinctively knows and adopts is most probably unknown to her counterpart in Karnataka who weaves her story in Kannada. There is so much diversity in Indian stories and often it is the very diversity that loops them together, sensuously, delicately, almost invisibly into something that looks whole to the outsider who does not see the woof and the warp, the brilliant colors that have been cajoled into each and every fiber by varying hands and minds.

In spite of interstate migrations within India, there are very few people who can read two or more Indian languages; and fewer still who would willingly take on the thankless job of translation. If this book exists today it is because of countless friends, acquaintances and friends of acquaintances who willingly and spontaneously helped. Most of these stories have been specially translated for this volume.

I'd like to thank U. R. Anantha Murthy, Asha Damle, G. P. Deshpande, Jai Ratan, Meenakshi and Sujit Mukherjee, Vakati Panduranga Rao, (Crea) Rama-krishnan, Shanta Gokhale, Surojit Banerjee, Uma Iyengar and her father, Shri Acharya, Varsha Das and O. V. Vijayan. And Shri Madan for his patient and careful typing of the manuscript. Also, Ratna Lahiri, without whose constant prodding and expressions of confidence this collection would not have seen the light of day at all. Raju, Tulsi and Guha, of course, have helped in more ways than they even know! This book is really for all three of them, with all the love that I can muster.

I'd like to present these as some of the best stories written in India in recent years. It is sheer serendipity that they happen to be by women.

New Delhi, 1991
GEETA DHARMARAJAN

INTRODUCTION TO THE
SECOND INDIAN EDITION

This book, published first by Mantra (U.K.), appears in this form for the first time in India. I feel that, in many ways, I have come a long way since then, maturing also (I hope!) as an editor. Rereading and re-editing these stories has brought back old memories, was fun. I would like to thank Rekha Mody of Garutmän for asking Katha to co-publish this book. I also have a very special word of thanks for Arvinder Chawla and Meenakshi Sharma; Guni and her two sons, Sasha and Ashu, good critics who questioned everything they could *not* understand; Ganeshan, for his eye for perfection; Suresh Sharma for his tolerance; Dipli, Poonam, Shalina, Reshma and the extended family at Katha for being there!

New Delhi, 1998
GEETA DHARMARAJAN

Separate Journeys

BAYEN

Mahasweta Devi
Translated by Mahua Bhattacharya

Bhagirath was very young when Chandi, his mother, was declared a bayen, a witch, and thrown out of the village.

A bayen is not an ordinary witch. She cannot be killed like an ordinary one, because to kill a bayen means death for your children.

So, Chandi was turned into a pariah and put in a hut by the railway tracks.

Bhagirath was raised, without much care, by a stepmother. He did not know what a real mother could be like. Now and then, he did get a glimpse of the shed below the tree across the field where Chandibayen lived alone. Chandi, who could never be anybody's idea of a mother. Bhagirath had also seen the red flag fluttering on her roof from afar, and sometimes, in the flaming noon of April, he had caught sight of her red-clad figure—a dog on her trail—clanking a piece of tin across the paddy fields, moving towards a dead pond.

A bayen has to warn people of her approach when she moves. She has but to cast her eyes on a young man or boy and she sucks the blood out of him. So a bayen has to live alone. When she walks, everyone—young and old—moves out of her sight.

One day, and one day alone, Bhagirath saw his father, Malindar, talk to the bayen.

"Look away my son," his father had ordered him.

The bayen stood on tiptoe by the pond. Bhagirath caught the reflection of the red-clad figure in the pond. A sun-bronzed face framed by wild matted hair. And eyes that silently devoured him. No, the bayen did not look at him directly either. She looked at his image as he saw hers, in the dark waters, shuddering violently.

Bhagirath closed his eyes and clung to his father.

"What has made you come here?" hissed his father at her.

1

"There's no oil for my hair, Gangaputta, no kerosene at home. I'm afraid to be alone."

She was crying, the bayen was crying. In the waters of the pond her eyes appeared to swim with tears.

"Didn't they send your week's ration on Saturday?"

Every Saturday, a man from the Dom community of the village went to the tree with a week's provision—half a kilogram of rice, a handful of pulses, oil, salt, and other food for the bayen.

A bayen should not eat too much.

Calling on the tree to bear witness, he would leave the basket there and run away as fast as he could.

"The dogs stole it all."

"Do you need some money?"

"Who will sell me things?"

"Okay, I'll buy the things and leave them by the tree. Now, go away."

"I can't, I can't live alone . . . "

"Who asked you to be a bayen, then? Go away! Go away!"

He picked up a handful of mud and stones from the side of the pond.

"Gangaputta, this boy . . . ?"

With an ugly oath Malindar threw the mud and stones at her.

The bayen ran away.

Malindar covered his face with his hands, and cried bitterly.

"How could I do it? I hurled stones at her body? It used to be a body as soft as butter. How could I be such a beast?"

It was a long time before he could calm down. He lit himself a cigarette.

"You, you talked to her, Baba?"

Malindar smiled mysteriously. "So what, my son?"

Bhagirath was terrified.

To talk to the bayen meant certain death.

The thought of his father dying scared the daylights out of him, because he was sure that his stepmother would throw him out.

Malindar said, his voice growing extraordinarily somber, "She may be a bayen now, but she used to be your mother once."

Bhagirath felt something rise to his throat. A bayen for a mother! Is a bayen a human being then? Hadn't he heard that a bayen raises dead children from the earth, hugs and nurses them? That whole trees dry up the instant a bayen looks at them? And Bhagirath—he, a live boy, born of a bayen's womb? He could think no more.

"She used to be a woman, your mother."

"And your wife?"

"Yes, that too," Malindar sighed. "It was bad luck. Hers, yours and mine. Once a bayen, she's no longer human. Which is why I tell you that you don't have a mother."

Bhagirath stared in wonder at his father as they walked back along the mud culvert. He had never heard his father speak in that tone before.

They were not ordinary Doms. They worked in the cremation grounds and the municipality allowed only one Dom family to work there. Malindar's family used to make bric-a-brac out of cane and bamboo, raise poultry on the government farms and make compost out of garbage. Out of the entire Dom community only Malindar knew how to sign his name—an accomplishment that had recently earned him a job in the subdivisional morgue, a government job that entitled him to forty-two rupees a month after signing on as Malindar Gangaputta. Besides, as Bhagirath knew, Malindar also bleached skeletons out of unclaimed bodies, using lime and bleaching powder. A whole skeleton, or even the skull or the rib cage, meant a lot of money. The morgue official sold the bones to would-be doctors at a handsome profit. The mere ten or fifteen rupees that his father got out of it was enough for him. He had invested the sum in usury and bought some pigs with the interest. His father was a respected man in the community. He went to his subdivisional office in shirt and shoes.

Red-eyed, Malindar stared at the red flag which burned above the bayen's hut like a vermilion dot against the saffron-colored horizon.

"She had everything, when she was your mother, my wife. I gave her striped saris to wear, and silver jewelry. I fed her, I rubbed oil into her hair, her body. . . . She used to be so afraid of the dark," he muttered. "Did fate have to make a witch out of her? She'd be better off dead. Did you know that no one can take her life except she herself, my son?"

"Who makes a bayen out of a person, father?"

"God."

Malindar glanced around wearily to see if any other shadow hovered near Bhagirath in the midday sun.

A bayen is crafty in her art like any flower girl in the market. If she is keen on having some child, she walks close by, her face in shadow in spite of the fierce sun all around. Invisible to mortals, she casts the shadow of her veil on the child as he walks. If the boy dies she chuckles with feigned innocence, "How was I to know? I just tried to make a little shade for him in the heat but then he goes and melts away like butter! Too soft!"

No, there was no shadow of a foul-smelling, filthy red veil anywhere near his son. "What is there to fear, my son?" he said. "She'd never do you any harm."

As days went by, Bhagirath's mind began to stray towards the hut. Be it on the paddy field, be it on the pasture with the cows, his mind would rush to the railway tracks, if only to see how terror-stricken the bayen was of her loneliness, to see how she put oil in her hair and dried it in the April wind.

He was too afraid to go to her.

Perhaps he would never come back if he did. Perhaps she would turn him into a tree or a stone forever. He only gazed out for days on end. The sky between the Chhatim tree and the bayen's hut seemed like a woman's forehead where the red flag—now limp, now flying in the breeze—burned like a vermilion dot. He had a mad wish to rush to the hut. Then, afraid of his own wish, he swiftly traced his way back home, wondering why no one mistreated him for being a bayen's son.

If you ill-treat a bayen's son, your children will die.

Bhagirath's stepmother didn't mistreat him either. In fact, she never showed any emotion for him whatsoever, the chief reason being that she did not have a son. Both her children, Sairavi and Gairabi, were daughters. She had no influence over her husband—first, because she hadn't borne him a son and second, because she had such protruding teeth and gums that her lips couldn't cover them. She would say, "My lips won't close at all. It makes me look as if I'm smirking all the time. See to it Gangaputta, be sure to cover my face when I die or else they'll say: There goes the bucktoothed wife of the Dom."

Jashi did nothing but work all day—cleaning the house, cooking rice, collecting wood, making cowdung cakes for fuel, tending to the pigs and picking lice out of her daughters' hair. She called Bhagirath "boy." Come eat, boy! Have your bath, boy!—as if theirs was a very formal relationship. If she did not take proper care of him the bayen might kill her daughters by black magic. Also, she knew she would have to depend on Bhagirath for support in her old age.

Sometimes she would sit, chin in hand, her lips baring her prominent gums, terrified that the bayen was working a magic spell on her daughters that very moment or making their effigies out of clay. At those times Jashi looked uglier than usual.

Malindar had deliberately married the ugliest girl in the community because when he had married the loveliest one, she had turned out to be a witch. Everyone knew that Malindar had loved his first wife deeply. Perhaps it was that love which had prompted him to tell Bhagirath everything about Chandibayen, his mother.

One day, they were walking along the railway tracks. Malindar had a parcel of meat under his arms. It was one of his strange weaknesses that he could not kill the pigs he raised himself. He raised them and sold them to others and when he needed some meat, he had to get a portion of the meat from his customer. "Shall we sit a while under this tree, eh?" he asked his thirteen-year-old son, almost apologetically. Then he sat down, his back against the trunk of the banyan tree.

After a while Bhagirath asked, "This is the place the robbers go by, isn't it, Father?"

Malindar liked to listen to him and often felt himself unworthy of his son.

Those days, the evening trains passing Sonadanga, Palasi, Dhubulia and other places were often robbed. They came in all shapes and sizes, these robbers . . . posing as gentlemen, poor students, refugees, settlers or houseowners, to get an entry into the compartments. Then, at a predetermined place and time they would pull the emergency chain and make the train stop in the dark. Their accomplices would rush in from the fields outside. They would loot all they could, beat up and even kill passengers, if necessary, before disappearing. This banyan tree, in particular, was their favorite haunt after dark. This is what made Bhagirath ask about the robbers.

Bhagirath went to the government primary school. Once, his teacher had made them paint the wall magazine. He had sketched out the letters himself and had made the boys color them. It was from the magazine that Bhagirath had come to know that after the Untouchability Act of 1955, there were no longer any untouchables in India. He also learned that there was something called the Constitution of India, which says at the very beginning that all are equal. The magazine still hung on the wall but Bhagirath and his kind knew that their co-students, as well as the teachers, liked them to sit a bit apart, though none but the very poor and needy from the "lower" castes came to the school. There are schools, and then there are schools. In spite of this, the fact was that Bhagirath now spoke a bit differently, his accent had changed.

But, Malindar's mind was elsewhere. His eyes scoured the bare fields and beyond, as if in search of something. "My son," he said, "I used to be a hard and unkind man, but your mother was soft, very soft. She cried often. What irony!"

Irony indeed! It was as if God came and turned the tables, in a single day, on the Dom community. Chandi became a bayen, a heartless childhunter. Malindar grew gentle. He had to. If one of a family turns inhuman and disappears beyond the magic portals of the supernatural, the other has to stay behind and make a man of himself.

Malindar grabbed his son's hand. "Why should you not know what everyone knows about your mother," he told him. "Your mother's name was Chandidasi Gangadasi, she used to bury dead children. She was a descendant of Kalu Dom. She belonged to a race of cremation attendants, the Gangaputras. They were known as Gangaputras and Gangadasis, men and women who cremated the dead ones on the banks of the Ganga. Any river was the Ganga to them, in reverence to the great river."

Malindar would carry bamboo trunks and slice wood in the cremation ground while Chandi worked in the graveyard meant for the burial of children, a legacy of their respective pasts. The graveyard lay to the north of the village, overlooked by a banyan tree beside a lake. In those days if a child died before it was five years of age, its body had to be buried instead of being cremated. Chandi's father used to dig the graves and spread thorn bushes over them to save the dead from the marauding jackals. "Hoi! Hoi, there!" his drunken voice would thunder ominously in the dark. Chandi's father survived almost entirely on liquor and hashish. On Saturday he would go round the village carrying a thali in his hand. "I am your servant" he would call out, "I am a Gangaputta. May I have my rations, please?"

The villagers were frightened of him. They would keep young children out of his way, silently fill his thali and go away. One day a fair girl with light eyes and reddish hair came instead of him.

"I am Chandi," she announced, "daughter of the Gangaputta. My father is dead. Give me his rations instead."

"Will you do your father's work then?"

"Yes. I will bury the dead and guard the graves."

"Aren't you afraid?"

"I am not."

The word "fear" was foreign to Chandi. She could understand why parents cried when their children died, but the dead had to be buried, they couldn't be kept at home. That was what her job was, simple as that. What was fearsome or heartless about it? It must surely have been ordained by God himself? At least the Gangaputras had no hand in it. Why should people detest or fear them so much?

This was the Chandi that Malindar was to marry.

Even in those early days, Malindar was in the bone-business with the morgue official. The bones from the charnel house were used as fertilizer and were expensive as well. Malindar had money as well as courage. At night he hurried to return home shouting across the field, "I am not scared of anybody! I am a fire-eater. I have no fear of anyone!"

One night he came upon Chandi, roaming alone, under the banyan tree, lantern in hand.

"Hey there!" he said. "Aren't you afraid of the dark?"

Chandi burst into peals of laughter which surprised him.

That very April he married her. The next April Bhagirath was born.

One day Chandi came back crying, carrying Bhagirath in her arms. "They have stoned me, Gangaputta, they said I meant evil."

"How dare they?" Malindar stopped fencing the yard and almost danced with rage. "Who dares stone the wife of Malindar Gangaputta?" he roared.

"Now, will you stop raising a row over it, and sit here for a while?"

"Oh, oh, oh!"

"Where is the shirt for Bhagirath?"

Malindar had forgotten.

"Tomorrow, I promise," he said. "A red shirt for my son, a red sari and a yellow blouse for the son's mother!"

"No, no, not for me. It only makes people envious and cast an evil eye."

"Don't I know that? At the primary school, they were always skipping classes. I alone learned how to sign my name. They were envious. I landed a government job, more envy. I married a golden doll of a wife, a descendant of the great Kalu Dom, still more envy. I built a new hut, and had two bighas of land for share cropping, how could they help being envious? Bastards! Get as envious as you like! I can take it all, I, Malindar Gangaputta. I'll send my son to school —over there, beyond the railway tracks."

As he spoke, Chandi who sat and looked fixedly at him, grew silent.

"I have not the heart to do it any more," she said at last. "I have not the heart to pick up the spade. But it is God's will. What can I do?" In wonder she shook her head and looked down at her limbs.

If there had been a male member of her father's family, he would have done the job. But there was none. She was a Gangaputra, keeper of the cremation grounds, She belonged to the family of the ancient Kalu Dom, he who gave shelter to the great king Harishchandra when he lost his kingdom. When the king became a servant, a chandal in the burning ghat, it was Kalu Dom who had employed him. When the king regained his kingdom and the ocean-girdled earth was his, he began to dole out large territories. "What have you got for us?" asked a voice booming large across the royal court.

It was the ancient Gangaputra. His type could never speak in a low voice nor hear one, because the fire of the pyres roared eternally in their ears.

"What do you mean?"

"You have ordained cattle for the Brahmins, daily alms for the monks. What have you for us?"

"All the burning ghats of the world are yours."

"Repeat it."

"All the burning ghats of the world are yours."

"Swear it!"

"I swear by God."

The ancient Gangaputra raised his hands and danced in wild joy.

"Ha!" he shouted. "The burning ghats for us . . . the burning ghats for us. The world's graveyards for us!"

Being a member of this particular race, could she, Chandi, reject this traditional occupation? Dare she, and let God wreak his wrath on her? Her fear grew greater every day. She would turn her face away after digging a grave.

Her fear and unease remained even after the grave was well covered with prickly bushes. At any time the legendary fire-mouthed jackal might steal in and start digging away with large paws to get at the body inside.

God . . . God . . . God . . . Chandi would weep softly and rush back home. She would light a lamp and sit praying for Bhagirath. At those times she also prayed for each and every child in the village that each should live forever. This was a weakness that she had developed of late. Because of her own child, she now felt a deep pain for every dead child. Her breast ached with milk if she stayed too long in the graveyard. She silently blamed her father as she dug the graves. He had no right to bring her to this work.

"Get hold of somebody else for this work, respected ones!" she said one day. "I am not fit for this any more . . . "

No one in the village seemed to listen. Not even Malindar, whose dealings in corpses, skin and bone—objects of abhorrence to others—had hardened him. "Scared of false shadows!" he had scoffed at her. If she cried too hard he would say, "Well, no one's left in your family to do this job for you."

It was around this time that the terrible thing happened. One of Malindar's sisters had come for a visit. She had a little daughter called Tukni who became quite devoted to Chandi. The village was suffering from a severe attack of smallpox at the time. Neither Chandi nor her people ever went for a vaccination. Instead they relied on appeasing the goddess Sheetala, the deity controlling epidemics. When Tukni got the pox, Chandi, accompanied by her sister-in-law and carrying the little girl in her arms, went to pay homage to the goddess. The temple of the goddess was a regular affair set up by the coolies from Bihar who had once worked on the railway tracks. There was also a regular priest.

As fate would have it, the little girl died a few days later, though not in Chandi's house. Everyone, including the girl's parents, blamed the death on Chandi.

"What, me?"

"Oh, yes, you."

"Not me, for God's sake!" she pleaded with the Doms.

"Who else?"

"Never!" she thundered out, "I swear upon the head of my own child that I've never wished any ill of Tukni, or of any other child. You know my lineage."

Suddenly those people, those craven, superstitious people, lowered their eyes. Someone whispered, "What about the milk that spilled out of your breasts as you were piling earth on Tukni's grave?"

"Oh, the fools that you are!" She stared at them in wonder and hatred.

"All right," she said after a pause, "I don't care if the rage of my forefathers descends upon me. I quit this job from this very day"

"Quit your job!"

"Yes. I'll let you cowards guard the graves. I have wanted to leave for a long time. The Gangaputta will get a government job soon. I need not continue with this rotten work any more."

Silencing every voice, she returned home. She asked Malindar if he would get a room at his new place of work. "Let's go there. Do you know what they call me?"

It was just to calm her down, just to pacify her with a joke, that he said with a loud laugh, "And what do they call you? A bayen?"

Chandi started trembling violently. She clutched at the wooden pillar that supported the roof. Excitement, rage and sorrow made her scream at him, "How could *you* utter that word, you, with a son of your own? Me, a bayen?"

"Oh, shut up!" Malindar shouted.

It was dead noon and the time for evil to cast its spell on human beings. It was a time when terrible rage and jealousy could easily take hold of an empty stomach and uncooled head. Malindar knew well the ways of his people.

"I am not a bayen! Oh, I am not a bayen!!"

Chandi's anguished cry traveled far and wide on raven's wings through the hot winds that reached every nook and corner of the village.

She stopped crying as suddenly as she had begun. "Let us run away somewhere when it's dark," she pleaded with him.

"Where?"

"Just somewhere."

"But where?"

"I do not know." She took Bhagirath in her arms and crept near Malindar. "Come closer," she said, "Let me lay my head on your chest. I am so afraid. I am so afraid to have thrown away my forefather's job. Why am I so frightened today? I feel that I'll never see you or Bhagirath any more. God! I am afraid."

It was here that Malindar stopped speaking and wiped his eyes. "Now that I look back, my son, it seems as if it was God who put those words in her mouth that day."

"What happened next?"

For a few days Chandi just sat as if dazed. She puttered about the house a bit and often sat with Bhagirath in her arms, singing. She burned a lot of incense and lit lamps about the house and had an air of listening closely to something or the other.

Two months passed by uneventfully. No one came to call Chandi to work. There had hardly been any work either. They lived very peacefully, the three of them. Chandi became whole again. "There ought to be some other arrangement for the dead children," she said. "The present one is horrible."

"There will be, by and by," Malindar said. "Things are changing."

"How am I to know if I did the right thing? You see, some nights I seem to hear my father raise his call."

"You hear him?"

"I seem to hear his Hoi, there!, just as if he were chasing the jackals off the graves."

"Shut up, Chandi . . ."

Fear grew in Malindar. Didn't he sometimes fear that perhaps Chandi was slowly changing into a witch? Some nights she woke up with a start and seemed to listen to dead children crying in their graves. Perhaps it was true what people were saying? Perhaps it would be best to go to the town after all.

The Dom community did not forget her. The Doms were keeping an eye on her, to her complete ignorance. Covertly or otherwise, a society can maintain its vigil if it wants to. There is nothing a society cannot do.

That's how one stormy night when Malindar was deep in drunken slumber, his courtyard filled with people. One of them, Ketan, an uncle of sorts of Chandi, called him out, "Come and see for yourself whether your wife is a bayen or not."

Stupefied, Malindar sat up and stared at them with sleep-laden eyes.

"Come out and see, you son of a bitch! You are keeping a bayen for a wife while our children's lives are at stake."

Malindar came out. He could see the burial ground under the banyan tree humming with lamps, torches and people who stood milling around in silence.

"Chandi, you!"

There she was, a sickle in her hand, a lantern burning beside her, a heap of thorn bushes stacked on one side.

"I was trying to cover the holes with these."

"Why, why did you come out?"

"The jackals had suddenly stopped their cries. Something in me said, there they are! Right at the holes, pawing for the bodies."

"You're a bayen!" The villagers raised their chant in awe.

"There is no one to watch over the dead."

"You are a bayen!"

"It's the job of my forefathers. What do these people know about it?"

"You are a bayen!"

"No, no, I am not a bayen! I have a son of my own. My breasts are heavy with milk for him. I am not a bayen. Why, Gangaputta, why don't you tell them, you know best."

Malindar stared, as if entranced, at the dimly-lit figure, at the breasts thrust out against her rain-soaked clothes. His mind was seared with pain, something whispered within him, "Don't go near, Malindar. Go near a snake if you will, a fire even but not now, not to her, though you may have loved her. Don't go, or something terrible will happen."

Malindar stepped forward and looked at Chandi with bloodshot eyes. He let out a yell like a beast, "O-ho-ooo! A bayen you are! Who was it in the grave when you were nursing with milk? O-ho-ooo!"

"Gangaputta! Oh God!"

The terrible cry that tore out of her seemed to frighten the dead underground, her father's restless spirit and even that of the ancient Dom, Kalu, whose cry would rend the sky and the earth when a human being was banished from the human world to the condemned world of the supernatural.

Malindar rushed to get the drum that had belonged to his father-in-law and ran back to the graveyard. He shouted as he beat the drum, "I, Malindar Gangaputta, hereby declare that my wife is a bayen, a bayen!"

"What happened next?" asked Bhagirath.

"Next, my son? She was forced to live alone at Beltala. As afraid as she once was to live alone, she is all alone now. Hush, listen how the bayen sings."

A strange strain of music floated up to them from afar, accompanied by the beat of a tin can. The song seemed to have no words at first but gradually the words became distinct.

> Come sleep, come to my bed of rags,
> My child-god sleeps in my lap,
> The elephants and horses at the palace gates,
> The dog Jumra in the ash heap.

Bhagirath knew the song. It was the song that his stepmother sang to make her daughters sleep.

The song entered his soul, mingled in his blood and reverberated in his ears like some inscrutable pain.

"Let's go home, son . . . "

Malindar led a dazed Bhagirath back home.

A few days later Bhagirath rushed to the dead pond at noon. He had heard the sound of the tin.

The shadow of the bayen trembled in the water. The bayen was not looking at him. Her eyes lowered, she was filling the pitcher.

"Don't you have another sari? Would you like a sari that is not torn like this one? Want my dhoti?"

The bayen was silent. She had her face turned aside.

"Would you like to wear nice clothes?"

"The son of Gangaputta had better go home."

"I . . . I go to school now. I am a good boy."

"Don't talk to me. I am a bayen. Even my shadow is evil. Doesn't the son of Gangaputta know that?"

"I am not afraid."

"It's high noon, now. Young children shouldn't be at large in this heat. Let the boy go home."

"Aren't you afraid to live alone?"

"Afraid? No, I am not afraid of anything. Why should a bayen be afraid to stay alone?"

"Then what makes you cry?"

"Me, cry!"

"I have heard you."

"He has heard me? Cry?" Her crimson shadow trembled in the water. Her eyes were full. Her voice cracked as she said, "Let the son of Gangaputta go home and swear never, never to come near the bayen. Or . . . or . . . I will tell Gangaputta!"

Bhagirath saw her turn back and race away along the mud culvert, her hair swirling about her face, her crimson sari fluttering in the air.

He sat alone for a long time by the pond, till the waters became still again. He couldn't recall the song.

On her part, the bayen sat in silence in her hut, thinking she knew-not-what. A long while later she raised herself and drew out a broken piece of mirror.

"I am only a shadow of myself!" she muttered incoherently. She tried to run the comb through her hair. It was impossibly matted.

Why did the child talk about nice clothes? He was too young then to remember now. What should it matter to him, good decent clothes for her?

She frowned hard in an attempt to collect her thoughts. It had been a long time since she had thought about anything. Nothing was left but the rustle of the leaves, the whistling of winds and the rattling of the trains—sounds that had muddled up all her thoughts.

Somehow she had a concrete thought today—the child was in for some terrible disaster. Suddenly she felt a very wifely anger at the thoughtlessness of Malindar. Whose duty was it now to look after the child? Who had to protect him from the witch's eyes?

She rose, lit a lantern and took the road. She hurried along the railway tracks. There was the level crossing, the linesman's cabin. Malindar, on his way back from work, would turn here and take the mud culvert. As she walked towards it, she saw them. There were people doing something with the tracks. No, they were piling up bamboo sticks on the tracks. The five-up Lalgola Passenger train was due that evening with the Wednesday mail bag. It meant a lot of money. They had been waiting for the loot for a long time.

"Who are you?"

She raised the lantern and swung it near her face.

The men looked up, startled, with fear-dilated eyes and ashen faces. She had never seen the people of her community look so frightened before.

"It is the bayen!"

"So you are piling bamboos, ah? You would rob the train, eh? What, running away from fear of me? Ha! Throw away these sticks first, or you are done for!"

They could not undo what had been done—clear the tracks, prevent the disaster. They could not. This is how society is, this is how it works. It was like when they had made her a witch with much fanfare and beating of drums.

The rain lashed her as she picked up the lantern. She was so helpless. What could she do? If she were a witch with supernatural powers, would not her servant, the demons of the dark, obey her bidding and stop the train? What could she do now, helpless as she was?

She started running along the tracks, towards the train, waving at it wildly in a vain bid to stop it.

"Don't come any further, don't! There's a heap of bamboo piled ahead!"

She continued to scream till the roar of the train drowned her voice and the train's light swallowed her up.

Chandi's name spread far and wide for her heroic self-sacrifice that had prevented a major train disaster. Even the government people came to hear of it. When her body left the morgue, the Officer in Charge, accompanied by the Block Development Officer, came to Malindar's house.

"The Railway Department will announce a medal for Chandi Gangadasi, Malindar. I know all about you, you see. She used to live alone, but there must be someone to receive it on her behalf. It was a brave deed, a real brave deed. Everyone is full of praise. She was your wife?"

Everyone was silent. People looked at one another, scratched their necks in embarrassment and looked down. Somebody whispered, "Yes, sir, she was one of us."

This announcement astonished Bhagirath so much that he looked from one face to another. So they were recognizing her at last?

"Well, the government cannot give the cash award to all of you at the same time."

"Give it to me, sir." Bhagirath came forward.

"And who are you?"

"She was my mother."

"Mother?"

"Yes, sir," said Bhagirath, and the officer started taking it all down. "My name is Bhagirath Gangaputta. My father, the revered Malindar Gangaputta. Residence, Domtoli, village Daharhati . . . my mother . . . ," he paused and then, very distinctly, "My mother, the late Chandidasi Gangadasi . . . (Bhagirath broke into loud sobs) . . . my mother, the late Chandidasi Gangadasi, sir. Not a bayen. She was never a bayen, my mother."

The officer stopped writing and stared first at Bhagirath, then at the crowd. The Doms stood silent, eyes downcast, as people condemned. The silence was suffocating and unbearable.

A Day with Charulata

Anupama Niranjana

Translated by Tejaswini Niranjana

The moment I alighted from the bus, my eyes went to the ridge of red earth. Everything seemed familiar—the banyan tree on the right, its leaves moving gently on the long branches; the sunlight making silver patterns on the stone ledge below, illuminating the intertwined images of cobras; the people sitting or sleeping on the ledge, or just walking by; those chewing betel nut and spitting out streams of red juice. All of them I was acquainted with. Through Charulata.

Even her name was beautiful. She had written only two novels, *The Mind's Bouquet* and *Face to Face,* and they had been acclaimed as great works of the period. For a long time I had wanted to write about this novelist and her life. Now here I was, searching for traces of Charulata in Sampigehalli, where she had lived fifty years earlier.

I turned left, and saw the Lakshminarasimha temple. The spire depicted the god Narasimha with his wife Lakshmi on his lap, surrounded by other gods, fanning of Sampigehalli scrambled all over the images, making faces at the passersby.

As if under a spell, I removed my slippers and entered the temple, more to see what Charulata had seen than out of piety. Inside was a simple courtyard, with a neat veranda of black stone, beyond which was the inner sanctum. The four pillars of the veranda portrayed Lakshmi, Saraswati, Parvati and Kali—Lakshmi's hauteur, Saraswati's radiance, Parvati's mercifulness and Kali's fierceness caught by the chisel in all their splendor.

"You seem to be a visitor. May I do an arati in your name?"

The priest, a thin young man in a dhoti and sacred thread, plunged into the sanctum without waiting for me to reply, performed the arati and brought the plate out to me. The face behind the burning camphor seemed vaguely familiar.

I took out a fifty paise coin from my purse and dropped it onto the arati plate. As if to get something for my money, I asked him whether he knew where Charulata's house was.

"Charulata?"

"She wrote stories. About fifty years ago . . . "

A memory flickered on his face. "Yes, of course. In my grandfather's time. Only her grandson Shankarayya is alive now. He lives right here. If you go straight and turn right, you'll see a house with Mangalore tiles which has four pillars, painted green."

He followed me out into the yard. "By the way, why are you looking for her? Are you a relative?"

I walked away without answering, leaving behind the question and the curiosity in his eyes.

It was getting hotter. There were only two small straggly clouds in the clear sky. On either side of the lane, several pairs of eyes had begun to watch me.

I found the house quite easily. It was the only tiled one there. As I approached, a young man of about thirty, clad in a shirt and dhoti, appeared. I introduced myself and explained the purpose of my visit. A look of surprise spread over his face.

"You want to write a book about my grandmother?"

"Yes. I'd like some information about her life."

"I don't know a thing. Never saw her. Only heard my father speak of her now and then. And even that I can't remember very well. Besides, I'm getting late. I have to be off to my fields."

Was there impatience in his voice? A kind of roughness?

"If I could speak to your father and mother . . . " I asked, politely.

"They died in an accident two years ago, on the way back from a pilgrimage to Tirupati."

I was disappointed. Would I learn nothing here?

Shankarayya turned to a woman who had appeared in the doorway. "Bhagirathi, this lady has came from the town. See if you can give her something to drink."

Tugging at the last thread of hope, I asked him quickly, "You do have a photograph of your grandmother in the house, don't you? And any old manuscripts . . . "

As if in anger, he said, "You're asking about someone who died years ago. Who keeps all that stuff? There used to be a couple of trunks in the attic . . . but I have no time now. If you come back in the evening, I'll have them taken down."

He walked swiftly away.

I sat on the mat Bhagirathi had spread on the floor. It was a large room, with neither light nor air. After a while, my eyes got accustomed to the dimness and began to discern the objects around. A big colored print of Lakshminarasimha. Perhaps their household god. A picture of a man in a turban and his wife, garlanded with a chain of kanakambara flowers, with incense sticks burning before them. Shankarayya's parents, obviously. An old-fashioned pendulum clock. A single chair. A bed on which bedrolls were piled. The inner door wore a handmade decoration, made lovingly by some woman of the house, with colored glass beads and tubes tinkling in the wind, catching stray slivers of sunlight. Perhaps Charulata had walked under it many a time . . .

Bhagirathi brought me dosa and chutney, and some coffee. She seemed rather shy.

"Have you read Charulata's novels?" I asked her.

"No. No one reads novels in our house!"

"Is there anyone from her generation in this village who's still alive?"

She wrinkled her forehead in an effort to remember. "There's an old woman called Sakajji. She may know something. I'll send our boy Sidda to show you where she lives."

"Charulata died very young, at thirty. Do you know why?"

"They say it was during childbirth, her second delivery."

Did Charulata write in this outer room? Had she used this chair? That bed? I went to the backyard to wash. The sight that met my eyes at once lit a brand in my brain.

Her own lines, from *The Mind's Bouquet* . . .

From the back veranda, I could see a beautifully shaped hill, its boulders gleaming black as though they had managed to lose the dirt of the world outside. Bursts of green amidst the rocks. Colored flowers like stars. There a passing cloud, here a bird in flight. . . . And then, suddenly, a troop of peacocks at the foot of the hill. When they danced with open wings for love of the gentle sunlight, it seemed as if heaps of gems sparkled, and the richness of life itself was spread out before me.

Had Charulata written these lines on *this* very veranda?

I sat down for a moment, until Bhagirathi called the boy.

I followed him. Huts of extreme poverty on either side, roofed with straw or palm fronds. Walls of mud, children in rags, old people with cataract eyes. One could see abundance too, in the green fields by the distant stream. This village, its turmoil, its passions, its hatred, its love . . . made splendid in Charulata's novels.

Sidda stopped in front of a hut by the stream. "Sakajji! Someone to see you!" he screamed.

An eighty-year-old woman appeared. Her build was slight, her face dried up and furrowed, her nose large.

> The most prominent feature in Sankamma's round face was her nose. She had a large black mole on her chin, and she touched her right ear now and then as she talked. Also, she would wave her hand occasionally and say, "Is that so?" Sankamma was a good friend, a compassionate woman. Unlike other people who wore no masks, she was undeceiving. (*Face to Face*)

Seeing Sakajji groping by the door, I realized she was blind. Was she really the model for Sankamma? Quickly, I told her who I was.

At once her face blossomed. "You want to hear about Charu, my dear? Come in, I can tell you plenty. We were best friends!"

I sat in front of the old woman, pen and notebook in hand.

"Look, for the last two years, I've had this film in front of my eyes and I can't see a thing. I told my grandson to have it removed, and he asked what an old woman like me needs eyes for!" She touched her right ear.

With some impatience, I said, "Tell me about Charulata. What did she look like? When did you first see her? How did you first become friends?"

Sakajji was silent for a while, as though she were gathering her memories together. Suddenly, she began to speak. "I first saw Charu when she came to this village as a bride. A tall girl she was. I remember the bride and groom were of the same height. She had long thick hair. Her face was somewhat long, and her eyes were big and black. She had a swift walk, and her laugh was like flowers breaking open. We were of the same caste, but not related, and we always met at weddings and other ceremonies. Since we were of the same age, we became friends. Whether Charu was happy, or sad, I would hear of it first. At that time, we had a big house with black tiles on the roof. We too lived well, until my son drank away all our wealth."

"Charulata had been to school, hadn't she?"

"She'd passed the class seven exams, and had even learned English. She knew the Ramayana and the Mahabharata well. She read a lot of Kannada books, and would tell me stories from them. Her aunt's son, Nagendrappa, used to bring her story books. She used to think very highly of him."

"Charu didn't talk much. We'd go to the temple together, at least once a week. After the puja, we'd sit on the veranda for a while and Charu would watch the people who passed by. Why do you stare so? I'd ask her. Look at all the kinds of people who come here, she'd say. Their clothes, their walk, their speech, their quarrels—how much you can learn from watching them! She would do the same at weddings. Wouldn't talk to anyone. People thought she was proud, because she was the daughter-in-law of a rich house. Charu's husband had had a great deal of jewelry made for her, but she didn't care for all that. Always surprised me. That girl didn't want anything."

A shadow fell across the doorway. Recognizing the person by the footstep, Sakajji said, "There you are, Seeta. See if there's any rice in the house. Make some for this lady. How can she eat only ragi and saaru?"

"I'm used to ragi," I said, not feeling good that I was causing them trouble.

Seeta set aluminum plates of ragi and saaru before us. As we ate, I asked, "Did Charulata's husband encourage her to write?"

Sakajji clucked. Her hand went to her ear again. "Oh no, he wouldn't do anything like that!" She raised her tumbler and drank the water steadily. "When he found out that she wrote stories he put all her papers in the wood stove, and then he took a brand from the stove and beat her. Charu came to our house, weeping. She stood before me, removed her pallav, and showed me the big red bruises on her back. . . . I had to turn away."

I, too, shivered. In front of me was Charulata, bending to show the bruises, earned for the sin of writing . . .

"She suffered a lot in that house, she did. Afterwards, she hid what she wrote. You tell me, what did she lack? She had plenty to eat, to wear. She could have been happy, if she'd been quiet, like other women. No, she didn't want that. She wanted suffering, she wanted her stories . . ."

After we'd eaten, Sakajji said, "Charu and I used to sit by the stream on the bank. She really liked that spot. Come, I'll show it to you."

Sakajji's gait was brisk, even more so than one who could see. I followed her slowly, stopping often to free my sari from the brambles. Reaching a rock, Sakajji sat on it carefully. "This is it," she said.

I sat down beside her.

In front of me the little stream sparkled clear. A branch of a large tree was bowed down over the stream and its image was etched on the water. In this calm atmosphere, the sudden cooing of a koel. Before I could raise my eyes to the tree, the bird was gone in a flurry of wings . . . (*The Mind's Bouquet*)

Nothing seemed to have changed. Nature was just as it was, while in the lives of human beings years had passed, bringing old age and weariness. Said Sakajji, "Charu wanted to know everything, Why is that so? Why is this so? She kept asking questions. The fights and quarrels of the village, the secrets . . . she wanted to know all about them. When I asked her what on earth she'd do with all this, she'd laugh like a child."

Should I tell her? I wondered. Ajji, your friend wrote about all these things. This village, this stream, this tree, this hill, these folk, their minds . . . she recorded everything, gave it to the world.

Sakajji sighed, placing her worn arm on my lap. "If she'd got the right medicine, Charu would have lived a few years longer. But her husband didn't want that."

"Shankarayya's wife told me Charulata had died in childbirth."

"That's a lie. She had an easy delivery, but the child died on the fourth day. After that Charu had a high fever. How much we implored her husband to fetch a doctor! But he wouldn't listen. For generations we've taken medicines only from our pandit, he said. For a week Charu suffered. And then, before our very eyes, she went away."

I thought Sakajji would cry bitterly, now that the dam had been breached. But I heard no sound. When I turned to look at her, tears were flowing profusely from her sightless eyes. With a heavy heart, I stood up. "Ajji, can you do me another favor? If you tell me in which town her aunt's son, Nagendrappa, lives . . ."

"Ayyo, child, he lives right here, by the temple. Ask for him by his name."

It was well past noon. The clouds were gone. There wasn't much movement in the lanes of Sampigehalli. Since I had to return to the town that evening, I walked swiftly.

The door to Nagendrappa's house was open. An old man of eighty-five or so sat reading in a chair on the veranda, and stood up as I approached. It seemed as if a coconut tree had risen. He was straight-backed and about six feet tall. Beneath his thick white eyebrows, his eyes were bright. His head was covered with white hair.

"Were you looking for someone?" he asked.

I explained why I had come.

His eyes became balls of light. A smile smoothed away his wrinkles. In a voice that was gentle and firm and gay at the same time, he said, "Did you say you want to write a book about our Charu? How happy she'd have been now if she were alive! Not even in her dreams did she imagine that people would be reading and discussing her books."

He pulled a chair forward so I could sit, and bustled about trying to make some tea. He said he had studied up to class ten. Unable to obtain a government job, he'd fallen back on farming. His children and grandchildren were in the city. "My limbs are still sound. I cook some rice for myself, and spend my time reading. I've always been crazy about books."

In front, there were two cupboards of neatly arranged volumes.

"Charulata must have been very fond of books too."

"Need you ask! Charu would have given her life for them."

Did his voice tremble when he spoke her name?

"I was the one who used to take books to Charu. Her husband didn't allow her to read them. So she'd read secretly. Her writing, too, was done in secret, whenever her husband was away. What suffering for a creative person! She'd send me what she wrote, and I'd post it to the papers."

He brought the tea and, as we sipped it, he continued, "When I went to their house, I'd go when he wasn't there. Although we talked only about literature, he was always suspicious. Charu had read all of Sharat Chandra, Bankim Chandra, Venkatacharya and Balaganatha. She constantly surprised me by her perceptive opinions of these writers. And she herself was a born writer. She used to say that given the leisure, thought and practice, she'd write better than any other Kannada author."

"How did her husband react to her first book?"

"That's quite a story. He didn't even know the book had been printed. The publisher came from the city with a sackful of copies, thinking he would sell some in the village after giving Charu her complimentary copies. Who knew how to read and write then? I was the only one who bought a copy. When the publisher had gone, Charu's husband found out about her book. He had always been quick-tempered. This time he took a piece of firewood and beat Charu as though she were an ox, saying she talked to every man she met. He threw all the copies of her book into the fire . . . "

Fifty years later, the scene seemed to evoke in him the old rage and regret.

"Charulata must have been greatly saddened," I said, thinking at the same time how foolish I sounded.

"Wasn't she! She cried and wept. Said she wouldn't write any more. But the following year she wrote her second novel, *Face to Face*. By the time it was published, she was no longer alive."

"Wasn't there a powerful reason for her to present the heroine of *Face to Face* as a rebel? I mean, when she couldn't rebel in reality, wasn't it a way out to depict the possibility in her writing? Sukhada, the heroine, runs away with the man she loves, unable to bear the cruelty of her husband, and faces the disapproval of society. Wasn't this attitude revolutionary for her times? Look at Charulata's discussion of love," I said, taking out a notebook from my bag and reading aloud.

Love is not a duty. It is a way of feeling, to be enriched by mutual respect and trust. There's no meaning in marriage and relationships without love. That's mere prostitution. Once love vanishes, it's not right that a man and a woman should stay together. Do you have the guts, then, to leave your husband? Why not? My life is mine. I seek to live only in the way I see fit.

"Yes. These are revolutionary ideas even today!" said Nagendrappa.

"Wasn't this novel reviewed at that time?"

"Where did we have book reviews then? Perhaps you mean an introduction to the work. In the monthly *Saraswati* someone called Neelakanta Dikshit wrote about the book. I should have a copy of the article somewhere."

After searching through the cupboards, Nagendrappa brought me a yellowing, crumbling magazine.

"*The Mind's Bouquet*—A Wonderful Work by a Woman Writer," proclaimed the title of the review. I started copying it into my notebook.

Shrimati Charulata, hitherto unknown, has raised a storm in the literary world with her very first book. Through its newness of content and its power of expression, this book disturbs our minds. It portrays the complexities of human relationships. Its uniqueness lies in its weaving together of nature and the human environment. Although Charulata has not stepped outside her little village, she is to be congratulated for having responded so intensely to her limited experiences to create such an excellent literary work. This writer has a brilliant future ahead of her.

"You helped Charulata in so many ways. She must have had great faith in you. Perhaps it was your friendship that prompted her to choose the subject of *Face to Face*."

He bowed his head. "I don't know. Charulata never revealed what she thought. In her situation, that was not possible."

"Did you love her?"

He lifted his head. His face had reddened.

The links in the chain came together. The dim picture looked clear now. The sun rose high in the heavens.

Seeing me stand up, Nagendrappa said, "You'll make Charu immortal!"

"I have no role in that. She's already immortal through her writing."

Leave-taking is always hard. Especially with people who have become intimate in such a short time. But I had work left to do.

When I reached Charulata's house, her grandson Shankarayya had returned from the fields. His face stern, he called to his wife to bring the trunk outside. She made an attempt to dust it, but traces of the years still remained on the lid. Inside was a faded photograph which seemed to have been removed from its frame just then. He handed it to me. Charulata's wedding picture. A girl of sixteen, covered with ornaments. Large black eyes, a longish face, a radiant but solemn expression—Sakajji's description come to life! Shankarayya tossed out a musty folded cloth with gold embroidery, now full of holes. Probably Charulata's wedding sari. The only other object was a rusted fountain pen. I wondered what else had been there and had been hastily removed.

"Will you give me this picture? And this pen?" I asked.

They had no need for them.

With care I placed the objects in my bag and stepped into the street, feeling light of heart. The little bird of Sampigehalli had been lifted out of its restricting frame and now was free to set off on a voyage around the world.

The bus was waiting and I got in. It moved westward.

The Decision

T. Janaki Rani

Translated by Vakati Panduranga Rao

Yes, someone was knocking at his door. At midnight! Who could it be knocking so loud that the dull hum of rain hadn't stifled the sound? "Who is there?" he shouted, as he got up and raised the wick in the kerosene lamp. "Who is there?" he repeated as he reached the door. The person on the other side continued knocking loudly. "Aiah? We are travelers Aiah, kindly open the door." It was a woman's voice. Ramakrishnaiah opened the door and in came two women as if blown in by the gale. One was middle-aged and the other was young and pregnant. The driver of a bullock cart followed, carrying a trunk and bedding.

The cart driver spoke, "These ladies alighted at the boat jetty when it was already dark, Aiah. So . . . "

"What made you start on a journey when she is so advanced in pregnancy, madam? That, too, in this rain and at this hour?"

The pregnant woman sat with some effort on the trunk. Her clothes were wet and water still dripped from her face. She leaned to one side and held on to her mother. "Amma . . . "

The elder woman ran gentle fingers through her daughter's hair. "My daughter has a vow to fulfill at the Devarapalem temple, Aiah, and her in-laws did not care to send her earlier. My son-in-law could not get leave from his office. By the time we reached your village, it had started raining. I begged the cart man here to help us. But, it was already midnight and we knew we couldn't make it to Palem. This is a big village, we thought we could seek shelter for the night in a house. So . . . "

The clock struck one. The rain outside seemed to have become weaker. He looked at the daughter who was leaning on her mother, her eyes half-closed. What was he supposed to do?

"Oh yes, most certainly, you are both welcome," he heard himself say "But then I am alone and . . . but, please make yourself comfortable."

Ramakrishnaiah went to his room. He lit another lantern. Except for the maidservant, it had been an age since his house had had a woman inside it and he just did not know what to do next. Two rooms, a veranda and a kitchen was all that his house had. He used one room for sleeping and the other was full of old, forgotten things. After a while, he pulled his mattress down from the cot and dragged the cot outside.

Would the women mind sleeping in the veranda for the night?

"Not at all, Aiah. We're sorry for this trouble. How can we ever thank you? We have our bedding, and can sleep anywhere," said the mother.

Ramakrishnaiah opened the kitchen door. He had kept some milk in a pitcher in the hanging rope-basket. He poured this into a glass, added a little sugar and brought it out. By that time the pregnant young woman was lying on the cot and her mother was sitting by her side.

"Please. . . . It must be quite some time since you ate."

The mother had stood up on seeing him. "You should not bother. I feel bad for all this inconvenience we are causing you."

Ramakrishnaiah stood silent for a minute, then slowly walked back to his room. He spread a mat on the floor and put a pillow on it. He dimmed the lantern and lay down.

What would the morning bring? That girl looked very exhausted, he thought. Could they travel another eight miles in her condition? I should ask the maid, Atchamma, to stay for a while and look after their needs because school reopens tomorrow and I have to be off early. What about their breakfast and other meals? He worried so, a million questions demanding to be answered, till, mercifully, sleep overtook him.

"Aiah, please, Aiah . . . Aiah!"

At first, he thought it was a dream, but there was someone moaning and that woke him up. He got up and came out of his room.

The older woman was all worked up. "Aiah, my daughter. She's started her labor pains."

"Oh God, what are we to do!"

"I am sorry," said the mother, her hands kneading her sari's pallav. "But, is there a midwife around, please . . . "

The daughter called weakly and the woman ran to her.

Ramakrishnaiah did not know whether he should follow her. Soon, she came back to say, "Aiah, if you do not mind, may we shift her cot inside? The veranda is open to the street."

He went in and folded his mat. Then he and the woman carried the cot inside together, with the pregnant woman wailing and moaning all the while.

"Will you please get the midwife?"

"Oh yes!"

He slung a towel across his bare shoulders and went out, saying, "Please bolt the doors."

It was four o'clock. A cock crowed, announcing the beginning of another day. The streets were full of puddles. Eighteen years ago, one night when Ramakrishnaiah's wife had had her labor pains, his brother-in-law had gone out on a similar errand while he had sat on the piol feeling helpless. Today he felt no different.

The midwife Lakshmi's hut was not far, but he had only once been to that side of the village. A school peon, living in one of those huts, had invited him to his wedding. That was four years ago. Now he stood outside his school peon's hut again.

"Ramulu!"

A wiry man came out and peered into the thinning darkness of dawn. "Oh, Aiah, it is you! What Aiah, what's happened?"

"Ramulu, midwife Lakshmi lives somewhere here, doesn't she?"

"Midwife Lakshmi, Aiah?" asked a puzzled Ramulu.

"Some travelers came to my house to rest and the woman is in pain. Lakshmi should be called immediately."

"You get back home, Aiah, I shall fetch her."

"No, I will wait here, get her at once."

The chorus of hens and cocks filled the air. A few people were up and about. It would be nice if the sun rises, thought Ramakrishnaiah.

At last they came. "You, too, had to come in search of me, Aiah," Lakshmi teased with an unexpected familiarity, her face wreathed in smiles.

Ramakrishnaiah smiled uncomfortably. He turned and walked briskly, leaving Ramulu to escort the midwife.

The door to his house was open and there were people running here and there. The lantern was burning bright. The mother came out and escorted the midwife in. The young woman was wailing loudly. Tremendous pity surged through Ramakrishnaiah as he and Ramulu sat on the piol.

"Ramulu, they may need hot water, why don't you call Atchamma?"

Two women came out—the wife of Avadhani, his neighbor, and her daughter-in-law.

"You could have called me and I would have sent my boy to fetch Lakshmi," said Mrs. Avadhani.

"It did not strike me at all. How is the girl?"

"She's fine. It's her first delivery, but her mother's very efficient."

Mrs. Avadhani had turned to go inside, then stopped. "They may be here for ten, fifteen days, but please don't worry. We are here to look after them. And the mother's a good manager."

Ramakrishnaiah settled down on the piol again.

"Kreeeer!"

A baby's first cry! Ramakrishnaiah was overwhelmed. That sound, in his house. He was amazed and afraid at the same time.

Midwife Lakshmi came out with a broad beaming face and announced, "Aiah, a girl, a Mahalakshmi is born under your roof. She is fair and . . . this big."

The rest of the day flowed past him like a dream. Without any effort on his part, everything went like clockwork. Food was served. Everybody had a bath except the young mother and her newborn who were fast asleep while Atchamma sat glued to the room. Ramakrishnaiah asked the old woman whether they had to write to anyone to tell them of the birth.

"I don't think so. Only my son-in-law needs to know and he is on tour somewhere up north. And my husband is too old to do anything. Anyway, we should be back home in another four or five days. We have already given you enough trouble," she said, and went in. She moved around the house as if she had been there for quite some time.

Ramakrishnaiah sat at his desk on the veranda. The meager provisions that he bought for himself were evidently exhausted. Earlier in the day, Parvatamma —the mother—had wanted a few things and was about to hand over a ten rupee note. He had declined the money and prepared a new list.

It was now the sixth day since they had first come. Every morning he woke up to the infant's shrill cry. Breaking his habit he came home from school at lunchtime on the second day, to find out if they needed anything. When he arrived, Parvatamma served him a minapa rotte and since then he always came home for his lunch which she would have ready for him.

He finished writing the list and estimated the cost. Not bad. He could manage without touching the amount he had saved for his pilgrimage to Tirupati.

"Aiah, Seeta and I plan to leave tomorrow," Parvatamma spoke, standing in the doorway.

He was startled for he had not seen her coming so near. Also, hadn't she just now asked him to get a few things?

"It is more than a week since we left and everybody at home will be worried."

He spoke hesitantly. "Can the mother and child be moved now, so early?"

Parvatamma just bit her lip. Finally, she went inside to bring him a cup of tea. Ramakrishnaiah sat looking at the list in his hands.

When she came back with his tea, she seemed to have reconsidered her decision. "I think we will do as you say. We will leave on the eleventh day, after my daughter is given the bath. I don't know how to thank you."

It was the eleventh day after the birth of the child. The day of the ritual first bath of the mother and child, the day the visitors would be leaving his home.

Ramakrishnaiah got up that morning to the incessant screams of the infant. He went towards the backyard. The kitchen door was shut and in the backyard firewood was burning under the big brass pot. The hot water for the ritual bath was ready.

He called out, "Atchamma . . . "

No one responded.

He helped himself to a little hot water to wash his face. The infant was still bawling.

He put down the small pot of hot water and came into the veranda. The lantern shed a dull light at the entrance to the room. The baby continued to cry. Her mother, was she in or not?

"Parvatamma gaaru," he called.

He raised the wick of the lantern and peeped into the room.

There was no one.

His heart beat fast.

On the cot was the crying infant and no one else!

The clock struck five. With lantern in hand he went to the front door and found it closed, but not bolted.

Ramakrishnaiah ran back to the room. The baby still cried.

He did not know what to do. What had happened to them? Where had they gone? Fear enveloped his mind like smoke from a smouldering fire. He stood staring at the screaming child.

"Aiah?"

It was Atchamma! Her voice came to him like a slender twig to a drowning man.

"Where is the baby's mother, Aiah?" She took the baby into her hands and it stopped crying at once.

Ramakrishnaiah shook his head and came out to the piol.

Avadhanulu was standing outside, washing his face.

"Do you know where these people in my house have gone?"

Avadhanulu turned white with disbelief. "What do you mean, I hear the baby crying. Are they not in your house?"

The panic was now a lump in his heart, growing heavier by the minute. No. They seemed to have left the baby and gone away. Not an item of their luggage was to be seen.

Mrs. Avadhanulu came out saying, "What is this that Atchamma is saying? Those women have disappeared leaving the baby, it seems!" Her son and daughter-in-law came out after her.

"Where did they come from?" asked Avadhanulu.

"The mother had said Rajamahendri. But who knows? This seems to be an illegitimate child."

Mrs. Avadhanulu had put into words the vague idea taking shape in everybody's mind.

Ramakrishnaiah looked helpless.

"Look here, you see to the needs of the baby," Avadhanulu said, turning to his wife.

Ramakrishnaiah went in and washed his face again.

Atchamma followed, baby in hand, saying, "Aiah, yesterday I found the young mother crying. That old woman was whispering into her ears again and again. She must have planned this dastardly act!"

Ramakrishnaiah put a vessel with water on the coal stove that Atchamma had lit to make a cup of coffee for himself. What was he to do with the child?

Atchamma appeared, to say, "Aiah, you must go and get a tin of milk powder and a feeding bottle."

Mrs. Avadhanulu came to tell him, "Since they said they came from Rajamahendri, why don't you go there and try to trace them? We will look after the baby for a day or two."

Ramakrishnaiah nodded his head slowly. He wished he could go with the baby, locate them and throw the baby into their laps, but . . . how could he take the baby? He would not even know how to carry her! And they, who had left the baby here, would they accept it? He looked at Mrs. Avadhanulu. Just because the child was born under his roof, these people seemed to imply that it was his responsibility to look after her. They would take care of her for just two days! Was not the baby the responsibility of the whole village?

He pressed his forehead hard with his palm.

Ramakrishnaiah applied for leave and sent the list to the shop. Mrs. Avadhanulu added a few more items to the list.

He reached Rajamahendri by three in the afternoon. He did not know where they lived. He did not even know Parvatamma's husband's name. Without any clues or direction he roamed around streets and lanes. Nobody seemed to know Parvatamma or Seeta. By six o'clock he knew it was futile.

And his feet burned from the unaccustomed walking in the sun the whole day.

As a last resort, he went to the railway station. He drank a bottle of soda and hailed a coolie and asked him if he had seen two women boarding the train. The coolie laughed and said, "Aiah, many fit that description!"

Ramakrishnaiah sat on a bench. The comforting buzz of the train, the hawkers' cries, passengers coming and going, talking, laughing. How nice it would be if he never had to go home again!

Next day, he took the early morning ferry to his village. His life had moved like the ferry, freely on the stream of life. Now, a heavy load had been added to it. It would have to sink, he thought. After he lost his wife, all these eighteen years someone or the other was always advising him to get married again. For as long as she had been alive, his wife had been sickly. Her sickness had drained his mind and life. When that fragile woman had died during her first childbirth, it was, in a sense, a relief. Her death freed him of all bonds. And he had been happy to live that way. Why did God want to bind him now? It was so unfair! By the time Ramakrishnaiah reached Avadhanulu's house the baby was happily asleep.

Avadhanulu said, "This child has come to you to collect the dues of a previous birth, friend. My grandson has named her Sasirekha. How do you like the name?"

Ramakrishnaiah did not know how, but that night was not the dark night he had feared.

Dawn brought another day. Sasi had been with them for a week without her mother. Ramakrishnaiah applied for a few days' leave and sat with her. Her suffering, his own agony, the effect of sleeplessness, the unending expenditure —it was all like a bad dream. But maybe Avadhanulu was right. He seemed to owe her all this attention.

Months passed. Ramakrishnaiah's mind rebelled at the thought that one single incident, not even of his making, had disturbed the entire course of his life, like a stone hurled at the placid waters of a pond. What harm had he done to them except that he had given them shelter when they had begged for it? They had cheated him. They had made a fool of him. They had played with his life.

At times, he felt so enraged that he was tempted to take the girl somewhere and leave her. But . . . but how? He told himself so many times that he could not stand her. She created one problem after another. If she was not picking quarrels with neighbors' children, she was falling sick, or coming home with absurd requests. He closed his eyes. Yet, he felt utter compassion when he looked into her eyes. But, she was tiresome.

The breeze coming over the hills was refreshingly cool. Ramakrishnaiah handed over his bag to the custody of the owner of one of the shops by the side of the bathing ghat of Pushkarani Pond. The ghat was teeming with men, women and children.

Suddenly, two days ago, he had felt a burning desire to see the deity at Tirupati. For how many years had he planned it, saved for it. He had left Sasirekha in the custody of the Avadhanulu family and come to Tirupati. He had been reading the Bhagavatam and the Bhagavad Gita from childhood, but had never understood their meaning nor experienced their ecstasy. Only now had he started enjoying them and deriving some peace of mind. His mind was becoming increasingly clearer.

He stood on the first step of the ghat and looked down to find a place for taking his bath.

Suddenly he saw her! Yes, it was Parvatamma.

Parvatamma, who was coming up the steps after her bath, spotted him. She stood frozen, then turned and hurried back towards the water. Ramakrishnaiah's heart hammered inside him. He too started down the steps but, seeing him following her, Parvatamma came up the steps towards him.

Ramakrishnaiah wanted to say a thousand things, speak of the agonies he had undergone during those two years. He wanted to shout at her, but not a word came out. He walked mechanically beside her. They reached a corner where there was no one.

Parvatamma controlled her sobs and said, "Ramakrishnaiah gaaru, you really are a god. You are our protector. My daughter is getting married tonight at the Tirupati temple."

Seething with anger, he asked, "Which daughter are you talking about?"

"Seeta, that wretched girl of mine. I am ashamed of it but I have to tell you. We both went to see my elder daughter who was ill and there, may his soul rot in hell, my son-in-law poured burning coals on the path of Seeta's life. We did not know till the fourth month. We were afraid that any step we might take would be extreme and would cost her her life. So we went away to Visakhapatnam and lived there for three months."

So it was true! But, coming from her it sounded strange to Ramakrishnaiah. His anger had calmed down.

"Even there, tongues started wagging. Ultimately, in the ninth month, the landlady asked us to vacate the house. I remembered your village which I had known in my childhood. We knocked on the first door and fortunately you opened it. I was certain that Seeta would not survive the delivery . . . "

She now made no attempt to arrest her tears. Maybe she was unburdening herself for the first time. She wiped her tears and spoke again. "It took me this long to find a good man to marry her. If we send her away to her in-laws tomorrow, she will start living her life like any other woman. It was a job these two years seeing that she did not jump into a well . . . "

Again her face was clouded with sorrow. "Seeta has been remembering you every day. Aiah, our lives are in your hands."

A deep sigh escaped Ramakrishnaiah. There was no way out of looking after Sasi. "You can go," he said.

"We are totally dependent on you. I shall redeem our debt in my next birth, Aiah."

Ramakrishnaiah could not help noticing the dignity in her face.

"The child, is she well?"

"She is fine. She turned two last month."

He turned abruptly and went towards the temple.

Never had he stood before the Lord with such an absent mind. In another two years he would have to retire. But Sasi had to be educated, then married off, now that it had been decided that she was his responsibility. He felt the tentacles of a worldly life encircling him in spite of his wish to remain aloof and alone. All along he had believed that someone would appear from somewhere or that some miracle would happen and the problem of the girl would be lifted from his aging mind. But no, today made it clear that all that was a fool's paradise. The die was cast.

"I have cleaned the lanterns and poured kerosene in them, Aiah. Now, I am going home."

Ramakrishnaiah nodded his head and went back to spinning yarn with a takli.

The door creaked and opened. The sound of chappals was heard and then a male voice said, "Shall I keep the luggage here, madam?"

Ramakrishnaiah adjusted his spectacles and looked up.

A woman came in carrying a boy. Another boy, a four-year-old, held onto the pallav of her sari.

"It is I, Aiah," she said gently.

Ramakrishnaiah had to come closer to see that it was Seeta.

After a minute, he managed to say, "Come, come and be seated." She was fair and dressed in a parrot-green silk sari and some jewelry, she looked handsome and dignified. After some minutes of silence he asked, "Where have you come from?"

"I have come for a wedding at Visakhapatnam. We now live in Madras. My mother might have told you."

"Go and wash your feet. There's some milk in the kitchen."

She got up, took out soap and a towel and, with one of the boys, started towards the backyard.

Why had she come now? Had she forgotten the circumstances of her last visit? And how dignified and confident she sounded. Sasirekha had not yet come home. When she did, how was he to tell her that this was her mother?

He was lost in thought. Meanwhile, Seeta came and sat down with a mirror in front of her. She unplaited her hair and started combing it. Suddenly she looked at him and asked, "Where is the child?"

How calm she was. Now after ten years she had at last come, to take her daughter back. It seemed as if a weight had been lifted off Ramakrishnaiah's shoulders.

"Yes, she is here."

He went out and stood at the doorway facing the street. He was reminded of that night when Seeta and her mother first came. When he went inside he found her sitting with her face resting on her raised knees. Her hair was still down. Her shoulders moved slightly. She was crying.

She looked up at him.

"Mama, is my child really here?"

He was surprised that she should call him Uncle.

"She has gone out to play," he said, curtly.

She looked at him. "I cannot live without her. How many times, since the day I left her with you and went away, how many times have I longed to come back. I want to take her with me, Mama. Not a day passes when I am not reminded of her. What sin did she commit to be left here? I know she is fine here but I need her, Mama, I need her."

Pity surged in him, thankfulness.

Sasirekha came running to Ramakrishnaiah and stood leaning on him, asking, "Grandpa, who is this?"

He did not look at Sasi but at Seeta. She was staring at her daughter with wide-open eyes.

Ramakrishnaiah blurted out, "Seeta Akka. Your sister."

"Come here, child," said Seeta. She embraced her and broke into uncontrollable sobs. Sasi stared at Seeta, puzzled.

Ramakrishnaiah's eyes, too, were filled with tears. His throat hurt. "Sasi, come here," he called, and the child shook herself free of Seeta's hands and came to him. He led her inside. He was brimming with ideas about what to tell her. Explanations and excuses rushed into his mind. "Akka was seeing you after a long time, so she cried. She is nice, isn't she?"

Nodding her head, Sasi left him to go to the backyard to wash.

What a striking resemblance the child had to her mother!

That night, ignoring his protests, Seeta cooked food. She herself sat beside Sasi as she was eating. She made her boy call Sasi, Akka. As she sat and coaxed Sasi to eat, he watched over them with affection. He felt happy for Sasi when the boys took out their toys and started playing with her. Sasi did not sleep till late in the night.

Ramakrishnaiah sat on the piol. After putting the boys and Sasi to sleep, Seeta came and sat before him. He did not know what to talk about.

"How is your mother?"

"She is very well." Seeta paused before asking, "Will you let me take Sasi with me?"

Her eyes had a peculiar glint which he was able to perceive in the light of the lantern.

The same question, again and again . . .

Who was he to send or not send the girl?

He spoke after a while. "What will your husband say?"

It seemed as if Seeta had been waiting for this question.

"Nothing. I will tell him that I found her, an orphan in a bus, or that she was lost and I found her. He will not utter a single word against my desire and decision. That has been my singular fortune."

That meant she had come with a well thought out plan. It looked as if she was the only one who had authority over the girl.

For quite some time no one spoke. His mind was heavy like a sky overcast with clouds about to give way. A long time ago, early one morning, when he saw a wailing infant in the hands of Atchamma, he had had that feeling. And today again . . . why?

"Seeta," he called. His throat was hoarse. "Seeta, do you know how cruel you both have been to me! You and your mother entered my life one night and left it totally in chaos. Did you ever feel even one day for my plight and suffering?"

"It will be hard for you to believe me if I say Yes, I have thought about you every day. More than you, it was the child whom I thought about and who dragged me here. You will never understand that. On that morning, as we were about to depart, she started crying persistently. Then I breast-fed her and made her sleep and went away with my mother. But the thought that when she cried next, I would not be there to wet her throat with my milk, that she would be crying like an orphan, that thought tugged at my womb. Mama, every nerve in me was on fire. Even today, after all these years, the pain is so intense, so piercing . . . " She was crying as she spoke.

Maybe. He didn't know. He got up. "Yes, you may take her with you," he said. He went to his room to sleep.

Seeta woke up in the morning and made coffee. She also served food by nine o'clock. After the meal Sasi packed all her clothes into a trunk. Ramakrishnaiah went to the shop and bought new clothes for Seeta, Sasi and the two boys. This was the last item of expenditure and with that he would be free from the debts of a previous birth, he felt.

Sasi, who was busy collecting all her odd belongings, suddenly came running. "What about you, Grandpa, aren't you coming too?"

He wanted to say No, but he checked himself. Somehow he felt like reassuring her. He said, "I will be there within ten days to get you back!"

She went away, chirping, merrily.

After fifteen minutes, he went out and returned with a bullock cart. Seeta kept looking at him and turning away. She never left Sasi alone that morning.

The cart man took up the trunk and put it in the cart. Seeta led the boy first to the cart and lifted him. She sat in the cart and then she stepped out again and stood before Ramakrishnaiah. Avadhanulu's wife and other neighbors had gathered to watch the proceedings.

"Mama, let me take leave of you. I will be writing to you. And don't forget to come to Madras to visit us. I gave you the address." Seeta's words came out as if in a hurry.

The cart man brought out Sasi's trunk. Sasi accompanied him. She caught hold of the edge of Ramakrishnaiah's dhoti. "Grandpa, you must come soon or else I will be missing lessons at school," she said.

Ramakrishnaiah's heart was like a load of iron. His breathing became heavy.

Seeta stepped forward towards the cart and said, "Come, come, Sasi."

As if someone had pushed him from behind, Ramakrishnaiah stumbled forward and took Sasi into his arms. "No!" he shouted. It was the first decision he was taking on his own, in many years. "Sasi, don't ever leave your grandfather and go away!"

PRIVATE TUITION
WITH MR. BOSE

Anita Desai

M r. Bose gave his private tuition out on the balcony in the evenings, in the belief that, since it faced south, the river Hooghly would send it a wavering breeze or two to drift over the rooftops, through the washing and the few pots of tulsi and marigold that his wife had placed precariously on the balcony rail, to cool him, fan him, soothe him. But there was no breeze. It was hot, the air hung upon them like a damp towel, gagging him and, speaking through this gag, he tiredly intoned the Sanskrit verses that should, he felt, have been roared out on a hilltop at sunrise.

Aum. Usa va asvasya medhyasya sirah . . .

It came out, of course, as a mumble. Asked to translate, his pupil, too, scowled as he had done, thrust his fist through his hair and mumbled, "Aum is the dawn and the head of a horse . . . "

Mr. Bose protested in a low wail. "What horse, my boy? What horse?"

The boy rolled his eyes sullenly. "I don't know, sir, it doesn't say"

Mr. Bose looked at him in disbelief. He was the son of a Brahmin priest who himself instructed him in the Mahabharata all morning, turning him over to Mr. Bose only in the evening when he set out to officiate at weddings, pujas and other functions. He was much in demand on account of his stately bearing, his calm and inscrutable face and his sensuous voice that so suited the Sanskrit language in which he, almost always, discoursed. And this was his son —this Pritam, with his red-veined eyes and oiled locks, his stumbling fingers and shuffling feet that betrayed his secret life, its scuffiness, its gutters and drains full of resentment and destruction. Mr. Bose remembered how he had seen, from the window of a bus that had come to a standstill on the street due to a fist-fight between the conductor and a passenger, Pritam slipping up the stairs, through the door, into a neon-lit bar off Park Street. "The sacrificial horse," Mr. Bose explained with forced patience. "Have you heard of Asvamedha,

Pritam, the royal horse that was let loose to run through the kingdom before it returned to the capital and was sacrificed by the king?"

The boy gave him a look of such malice that Mr. Bose bit the end of his moustache and fell silent, shuffling through the pages. "Read on, then," he mumbled, and listened for a while, as Pritam blundered heavily through the Sanskrit verses that rolled off his father's experienced tongue, and even Mr. Bose's shy one, with such rich felicity. When he could not bear it any longer, he turned his head, slightly, just enough to be able to look out of the corner of his eye through the open door, down the unlit passage at the end of which, in the small dimly-lit kitchen, his wife sat kneading dough for purees, their child at her side. Her head was bowed so that some of her hair had freed itself of the long steel pins he hated so much and hung about her pale, narrow face. The red border of her sari was the only strip of color in that smoky scene. The child beside her had his back turned to the door so that Mr. Bose could see his little brown buttocks under the short white shirt, squashed firmly down upon the woven mat. Mr. Bose wondered what it was that kept him so quiet— perhaps his mother had given him a lump of dough to mold into some thick and satisfying shape. Both of them seemed bound together and held down in some deeply absorbing act from which he was excluded. He would have liked to break in and join them.

Pritam stopped reading, maliciously staring at Mr. Bose whose lips were wavering into a smile beneath the ragged moustache. The woman, disturbed by the break in the recitation on the balcony, looked up, past the child, down the passage and into Mr. Bose's face. Mr. Bose's moustache lifted up like a pair of wings and, beneath them, his smile lifted up and out with almost a laugh of tenderness and delight. Beginning to laugh herself, she quickly turned, pulled down the corners of her mouth with mock sternness, trying to recall him to the path of duty, and picking up a lump of sticky dough, handed it back to the child, softly urging him to be quiet and let his father finish the lesson.

Pritam, the scabby, oil-slick son of a Brahmin priest, coughed theatrically —a cough imitating that of a favorite screen actor, surely, it was so false and exaggerated and suggestive. Mr. Bose swung around in dismay, crying, "Why have you stopped? Go on, go on."

"You weren't listening, sir."

Many words, many questions leapt to Mr. Bose's lips, ready to pounce on this miserable boy whom he could hardly bear to see sitting beneath his wife's holy tulsi plant that she tended with prayers, water-can and oil-lamp every evening. Then, growing conscious of the way his moustache was quivering upon his upper lip, he said only, "Read."

Ahar va asvam purustan mahima nvajagata . . .

Across the road someone turned on a radio and a song filled with a pleasant lilting weltschmerz twirled and sank, twirled and rose from that balcony to this. Pritam raised his voice, grinding through the Sanskrit consonants like some dying, diseased tramcar. From the kitchen only a murmur and the soft thumping of the dough in the pan could be heard—sounds as soft and comfortable as sleepy pigeons. Mr. Bose longed passionately to listen to them, catch every faint nuance, but to do this he would have to smash the radio, hurl the Brahmin's son down the iron stairs. . . . He curled up his hands on his knees and drew his feet together under him, horrified at this welling up of violence inside him, under his pale pink bush-shirt, inside his thin, ridiculously heaving chest. As often as Mr. Bose longed to alter the entire direction of the world's revolution, as often as he longed to break the world apart into two halves and shake out of them—What? Festival fireworks, a woman's soft hair, blood-stained feathers?—he would shudder and pale at the thought of his indiscretion, his violence, this secret force that now and then threatened, clamored, so that he had quickly to still it, squash it. After all, he must continue with his private tuitions, that was what was important. The baby had to have his first pair of shoes and soon he would be needing oranges, biscuits, plastic toys. "Read," said Mr. Bose, a little less sternly, a little more sadly.

But, "It is seven, I can go home now," said Pritam triumphantly, throwing his father's thick yellow Mahabharata into his bag, knocking the bag shut with one fist and preparing to fly.

Where did he fly to? Mr. Bose wondered if it would be the neon-lit bar off Park Street. Then, seeing the boy disappear down the stairs—the bulb had fused again—he felt it didn't matter, didn't matter one bit since it left him alone to turn, plunge down the passage and fling himself at the doorposts of the kitchen, there to stand and gaze down at his wife, now rolling out purees with an exquisite, back-and-forth rolling motion of her hands, and his son, trying now to make a spoon stand on one end.

She only glanced at him, pretended not to care, pursed her lips to keep from giggling, flipped the puree over and rolled it finer and flatter still. He wanted so much to touch her hair, the strand that lay over her shoulder in a black loop, and did not know how to—she was so busy. "Your hair is coming loose," he said.

"Go, go," she warned, "I hear the next one coming."

So did he. He heard the soft patting of sandals on the worn steps outside. So all he did was bend and touch the small curls of hair on his son's neck. They were so soft, they seemed hardly human and quite frightened him. When he took his hand away he felt the wisps might have come off onto his fingers and he rubbed the tips together wonderingly The child let the spoon fall, with a magnificent ring, onto a brass dish and started at this discovery of percussion.

The light on the balcony was dimmed as his next pupil came to stand in the doorway. Quickly he pulled himself away from the doorpost and walked back to his station, tense with unspoken words and unexpressed emotion. He had quite forgotten that his next pupil, this Wednesday, was to be Upneet. Rather Pritam again than this once-a-week typhoon, Upneet of the floral sari, ruby earrings and shaming laughter. Under this Upneet's gaze such ordinary functions of a tutor's life as sitting down at a table, sharpening a pencil and opening a book to the correct page became matters of farce, disaster and hilarity. His very bones sprang out of joint. He did not know where to look—everywhere were Upneet's flowers, Upneet's giggles. Immediately, at the very sight of the tip of her sandal peeping out beneath the floral hem of her sari, he was a man broken to pieces, flung this way and that, rattling. Rattling.

Throwing away the Sanskrit books, bringing out volumes of Bangla poetry, opening to a poem by Jibanandan Das, he wondered ferociously: Why did she come? What use had she for Bangla poetry? Why did she come from that house across the road where the loud radio rollicked, to sit on his balcony, in view of his shy wife, making him read poetry to her? It was intolerable. Intolerable, all of it—except, only for the seventy-five rupees paid at the end of the month. Oranges, he thought grimly, and milk, medicines, clothes. And he read to her:

> Her hair was the dark night of Vidisha,
> Her face, the sculpture of Svarasti . . .

Quite steadily he read, his tongue tamed and enthralled by the rhythm of the verse he had loved (copied on a sheet of blue paper, he had sent it to his wife one day when speech proved inadequate).

> "Where have you been so long?" she asked,
> Lifting her bird's nest eyes,
> Banalata Sen of Natore.

Pat-pat-pat. No, it was not the rhythm of the verse, he realized, but the tapping of her foot, green-sandaled, red-nailed, swinging and swinging to lift the hem of her sari up and up. His eyes slid off the book, watched the floral hem swing out and up, out and up as the green-sandaled foot peeped out, then in, peeped out, then in. For a while his tongue ran on of its own volition:

> All birds come home, and all rivers,
> Life's ledger is closed . . .

But he could not continue—it was the foot, the sandal that carried on the rhythm exactly as if he were still reciting. Even the radio stopped its rollicking and, as a peremptory voice began to enumerate the day's disasters and achievements all over the world, Mr. Bose heard more vigorous sounds from his kitchen as well. There, too, the lulling pigeon sounds had been crisply turned off and what he heard were bangs and rattles among the kitchen pots, a kettledrum of commands, he thought. The baby, letting out a wail of surprise, paused, heard the nervous commotion continue and intensify and launched himself on a series of wails.

Mr. Bose looked up, aghast. He could not understand how these two halves of the difficult world that he had been holding so carefully together, sealing them with reams of poetry, reams of Sanskrit, had split apart into dissonance. He stared at his pupil's face—creamy, feline, satirical—and was forced to complete the poem in a stutter:

> Only darkness remains, to sit facing
> Banalata Sen of Natore.

But the darkness was filled with hideous sounds of business and anger and command. The radio news commentator barked, the baby wailed, the kitchen pots clashed. He even heard his wife's voice raised, angrily, at the child, like a threatening stick. Glancing again at his pupil whom he feared so much, he saw precisely that lift of the eyebrows and that twist of a smile that disjointed him, rattled him.

"Er . . . please read," he tried to correct, to straighten, that twist of eyebrows and lips. "Please read."

"But you have read it to me already," she laughed, mocking him with her eyes and laugh.

"The next poem," he cried, "read the next poem," and turned the page with fingers as clumsy as toes.

"It is much better when you read to me," she complained impertinently, but read, keeping time to the rhythm with that restless foot which he watched as if it were a snake charmer's pipe, swaying. He could hear her voice no more than the snake could the pipe's—it was drowned out by the baby's wails, swelling into roars of self pity and indignation in this suddenly hard-edged world.

Mr. Bose threw a piteous, begging look over his shoulder at the kitchen. Catching his eye, his wife glowered at him, tossed the hair out of her face and cried, "Be quiet, be quiet, can't you see how busy your father is?" Red-eared, he turned to find Upneet looking curiously down the passage at this scene of domestic anarchy, and said, "I'm sorry, sorry . . . please read."

"I have read!" she exclaimed. "Didn't you hear me?"

"So much noise—I'm sorry," he gasped and rose to hurry down the passage and hiss, pressing his hands to his head as he did so, "Keep him quiet, can't you? Just for half an hour!"

"He is hungry," his wife said, as if she could do nothing about that.

"Feed him then," he begged.

"It isn't time," she said angrily.

"Never mind. Feed him, feed him."

"Why? So that you can read poetry to that girl in peace?"

"Shh!" he hissed, shocked, alarmed that Upneet would hear. His chest filled with the injustice of it. But this was no time for pleas or reason. He gave another desperate look at the child who lay crouched on the kitchen floor, rolling with misery. When he turned to go back to his pupil, who was watching them with interest, he heard his wife snatch up the child and tell him, "Have your food then, have it and eat it—don't you see how angry your father is?"

He spent the remaining half-hour with Upneet, trying to distract her from observing his domestic life. Why should it interest her? he thought angrily. She came here to study, not to mock, not to make trouble. He was her tutor, not her clown! Sternly, he gave her dictation but she was so hopeless—she learned no Bangla at her convent school, found it hard even to form the letters of the Bangla alphabet—that he was left speechless. He crossed out her errors with his red pencil—grateful to be able to cancel out, so effectively, some of the ugliness of his life—till there was hardly a word left uncrossed and, looking up to see her reaction, found her far less perturbed than he. In fact, she looked quite mischievously pleased. Three months of Bangla lessons to end in this! She was as triumphant as he was horrified. He let the red pencil fall with a discouraged gesture. So, in complete discord, the lesson broke apart, they all broke apart and for a while Mr. Bose was alone on the balcony, clutching at the rails, thinking that these bars of cooled iron were all that were left for him to hold. Inside, all was a conflict of shame and despair, in garbled grammar.

But, gradually, the grammar rearranged itself according to rule, corrected itself. The composition into quiet made quite clear the exhaustion of the child, asleep or nearly so. The sounds of dinner being prepared were calm, decorative even. Once more the radio was tuned to music, sympathetically sad. When his wife called him in to eat, he turned to go with his shoulders beaten, sagging, an attitude repeated by his moustache.

"He is asleep," she said, glancing at him with a rather ashamed face, conciliatory.

He nodded and sat down before his brass tray. She straightened it nervously, waved a hand over it as if to drive away a fly he could not see, and turned to the fire to fry hot purees for him, one by one, turning quickly to heap them on his tray so fast that he begged her to stop.

"Eat more," she coaxed. "One more," as though the extra puree were a peace offering following her rebellion of half an hour ago. He took it with reluctant fingers but his moustache began to quiver on his lip, as if beginning to wake up. "And you?" he asked. "Won't you eat now?"

About her mouth, too, some quivers began to rise and move. She pursed her lips, nodded and began to fill her tray, piling up the purees in a low stack.

"One more," he told her. "Just one more," he teased, and they laughed.

THE EMPTY CHEST

Mamoni Raisom Goswami

Translated by Pradipta Borgohain

No one got up at this hour, not even the people who had come to live on the fringes of the cremation ground. A few bulbuls chattered in the hijol tree in front of Toradoi's shack. A flock of yellow-billed garubok had just flown past, heading for the horizon to the east of the Brahmaputra. The stench of burnt human flesh stole across the cremation ground to mingle with the sweet scent of distant lemon blossoms.

As she came out of her shack, Toradoi saw Haibor, the firewood vendor from the crematory, standing under the hijol tree. Again! His spindly legs stuck out from beneath his black shorts. His white teeth gleamed like the hewed-up remains of sugarcane sticks.

Toradoi darted back into the house.

"What is left in this body to keep drawing you here?" she muttered. "Why don't you leave me in peace?"

How well she remembered his words. They fell on her ears again, like hammer-blows. "It will be a long time before that drunkard of yours comes out of jail. That is, if he ever comes out! After all, he has killed not one, but two people by running them over. It has been proved that he was drunk while driving. But I am here, don't worry! I will help, just keep your door open at night. This way, at least your two children won't starve to death!" Haibor had said. Since then, lured by the prospect of seeing Toradoi's door open to him, Haibor would come, even before daybreak, to stand under the hijol tree where the birds chirped and sipped honey from the flowers above his head.

When finally Toradoi went out again and looked around, Haibor was nowhere in sight. No, the firewood vendor was not one of those who came furtively to see the wooden chest she had scavenged from the cremation ground. She peered around. Was someone still prying?

What kind of people were these who liked to sniff at each other the way starving dogs do? Shameless bastards! As if they would not strip you naked if they could. The zamindar of Chakroad had died just the other day. Now, doesn't chowkidar Haladhar's hag of a wife sleep on the zamindar's bed made of uriam wood? And doesn't woodcutter Sukura's wife puff away at the hookah scrounged from this cremation ground? Some people had even salvaged gold rings from the charred remains of cremated bodies, but no, no one kept track of *those* things. No one had the morbid curiosity to see how Haladhar's specter-like wife slept on the zamindar's bed. The belongings of the dead lay scattered in all the shacks and shanties in and around the crematorium. Various opulent objects leered from these incongruous settings. Yet all eyes were only on this black box of hers!

Toradoi returned to her shack. Her eyes fell on her sleeping children. One could count their ribs. Their trousers hung loose like the hides of goats strung up in a butcher's shop. But there, next to them, lay the wooden chest! Its very existence gave strength to Toradoi. She ran her hands over the chest, caressing it. The bakul flowers, beautifully engraved on its sides, seemed real. She pressed her cheek to the flowers. Then, as on other days, she wriggled into the huge chest and lay there, leaving its cavernous mouth open.

Strange! Strange indeed! Reveling in the incomparable pleasure she felt, Toradoi lay inert for a long time in this chest which had been flung aside after it had been divested of its dead passenger. When she had scrounged the chest from the cremation ground she had had to take some bloodstained pieces of ice out of it. She had almost forgotten about that. Toradoi wept.

After some time, a police jeep roared past her hut. No vehicles other than police ones passed this way, usually. Were the certificates concerning the handing over of the bodies of people killed in the shooting in order? Was it true as the chowkidar's report would have it, that someone had burned a bastard child here without obtaining a "hand-over" certificate? And what about the unregistered corpses? Such were the matters that drew the police to this area. These and the trade of the prostitutes of Satgaon that flourished here. It almost seemed as if the higher the flames devouring the dead rose, the greater was the heat generated by the bodies of these prostitutes. Yes, there were so many things that the police had to attend to, so many matters that ensured a continual movement of police cars, that led to altercations between the police and members of the crematorium committee.

Toradoi woke up with a start at the sound of the police jeep. Vermilion and flowers, which were meant for decorating one's hair, lay scattered inside the chest. Strange! How had her very being become so inextricably entangled with this inanimate chest? She felt she was spending the night on the same bed with the "adored one." This wooden chest bore the imprints of her personality —her hair, oil, vermilion. Last night, she had again taken her wedding blouse from the pile of tattered clothes and put it on. It was the only piece of her clothing which was still intact. Looking at her reflection in the mirror in the flickering light of a kerosene lamp, she had combed her hair with frantic eagerness, as she had done ten years ago. She had not even felt the comb grate against the bones on her shoulder and neck. In those days she had hardly been aware of the existence of bones, buried as they were under her pliant flesh. Now people counted her amongst the numerous living skeletons who lived off the cremation ground.

Was anyone looking?

These days people peeped through crannies and gaps between doors and windows and walls. Her boys, now sleeping peacefully, had complained that people spied all the time. "Shame, shame! Sleeping in the box that carried the dead! Throw it away!" the voices seemed to say.

Toradoi snuggled into the chest. This experience was unique.

Suddenly, someone gave a massive kick to the door. Startled and flustered, Toradoi got up. Straining her ears, she heard the booming voice of her brother, Someswar, who worked in the police. "Toradoi! Toradoi!"

As soon as Toradoi opened the door a man dressed in police uniform burst in. Sturdily built, he had an imposing moustache. He wore a pair of huge un-gainly boots and carried a sizeable stick.

"I haven't been able to find the time to see how you are. Today my duty was in these parts. That woman from Satgaon has virtually set up shop here. It seems virtue is totally extinct. The other day Barua died and his two sons brought his body to the crematory. While one was busy performing the last rites, the other slipped out and was in that prostitute's room in a flash. Really, we have fallen on evil days!"

Suddenly Someswar gasped and retreated a few steps, as if he had seen a snake. He gaped at the massive, elaborately decorated wooden chest. Going closer, he tapped it with his stick. Then he walked around it. Finally, he knelt down by its side and, taking out a handkerchief, rubbed his eyes. The man who had rushed in like a storm a few moments before now resembled a dejected and defeated soldier.

He looked at Toradoi and asked in a broken voice, "Is there some water in the house? Get me a glass of water, will you?"

He gulped down the water and then said, his head downcast, "What I heard is true, then. Saru Bopa's corpse traveled here in this chest. I accompanied the family part of the way from the airport. Yes, this is that chest, all right."

With a level and direct look at Toradoi, he continued, "Don't think I don't remember that you worked for them. Everyone knows what a great help you were when Saru Bopa's father, the Thakur, was ill. Washing all those clothes stained with blood and pus. And Saru Bopa?" Someswar's voice grew heavy with emotion. "He was so fond of you. Wasn't that the time when he was bent on marrying you? What a fracas there was in the Thakur's household over this! Then came the hasty transfer to Upper Assam . . . and then, the accident."

Toradoi asked suddenly, "What killed him?"

"A jeep. What a fine figure of a man he was! After removing the blood-stained pieces of ice, I had helped hoist his body on to the funeral pyre. With these two hands of mine. Fresh young blood on my hands . . . " Looking at Toradoi standing like a statue, he could not complete his sentence. The big, black box with its open mouth was like some mysterious cave, separating and alienating the two from each other.

All of a sudden Someswar stood up and bellowed. There was a hint of the theatrical in his gesture. "Toradoi, the days of sahibs marrying the daughters of laborers are gone. The grass now grows tall over the bones of Jenkins Sahib who married a laborer's girl. The big sahib's son, Saru Bopa, vowed he would marry you. But could he do it? Was he able to take you away from this hovel and give you a place in a house with a tin roof?"

A sigh that seemed to wrack her whole being escaped Toradoi. "He stayed a bachelor only because he couldn't marry me. For twelve whole years. He would have probably never married at all."

The huge constable glared at Toradoi. Beating a staccato note on the floor with his stout lathi he stood up, cursing Toradoi in a deep, rumbling voice, "You are still as much of an idiot now as you were when you gave yourself completely to the Thakur's son. I work in the police, so I have heard everything and have come prepared."

Toradoi looked helplessly at her brother. She had managed to salvage something precious from the ruins of what had once been. Would her brother deprive her of even that?

By this time the sleeping children had got up. The three of them—Toradoi and her sons—huddled together, looking like phantoms from the cremation ground. Someswar started rummaging in his pocket. The boys thought he was going to come up with something for them, like that man who always waited for their mother did. After all, he was their uncle, though he had not once come to inquire after them when their father went to jail.

The three continued to stare at Someswar. Toradoi could almost hear her own heartbeat.

Someswar dug out a bundle of letters from his pocket and flung them in her face. "Here, take his wedding cards," he declared. "Seeing the way things have been, I came prepared. Saru Bopa was not planning to stay an eternal bachelor because of you. His wedding had been fixed. Cards had also been printed.

Read them. Read them! In fact he was on his way home to get married when the accident happened. Read them and pray for the peace of his soul."

As he was about to rush out of the room, he suddenly noticed the boys clinging to their mother. He searched for some coins, but his mind was already on other things. Toradoi could hear him mutter, "If I find that woman who peddles her body to mourners or catch Haibor red-handed, I can make this trip worthwhile. That bastard Haibor passes off worm-eaten wood as sal wood."

Taking out a fistful of coins, Someswar thrust them into the eager hands of the boys and left the way he had come. The moment their fingers closed around the coins, the half-starved urchins streaked off to the nearest shop.

Toradoi remained rooted to the spot near the pile of wedding cards. She reached out for them like one who gropes for the bones of the dead in the ashes at a crematorium. Yes indeed, they were invitations to a wedding.

Toradoi did not venture out for many days. Tormented by unbearable hunger, her sons were driven to beg from the people who came to burn bodies. Someone had tied a gamosa—which must have been worn by some person performing last rites—around the younger boy's head. The boys had managed to scavenge two empty liquor bottles from the cremation ground. They had washed these and filled them with water from the well near the statue of Yama astride a buffalo, and this they drank to quench their hunger. The neighbors knew that Toradoi's hearth was cold.

The big black chest lay with its mouth yawning open like the cavernous mouth of hell.

Under the hijol tree Haibor kept up his unceasing vigil.

One morning, while the gloom of night still clung to the sky, Toradoi and her two sons could be seen dragging the wooden chest towards the cremation ground. Toradoi put the box at the spot where the bastard child had been controversially burned. She set fire to it.

The bulbuls on the hijol tree started chirping noisily. The sun rose above the Brahmaputra. Wreaths of violet and brown clouds clung to it, making it look like the pinched and pale face of a hapless prostitute, blushing at the thought of having to spend time with an unwanted stranger. The clouds seemed to lay bare the strange combination of helplessness and indomitable strength on this face.

The cinders of the burned out chest were scattered all over the place. In the morning sunshine it resembled the hide of a freshly butchered goat, spread out on the earth to dry.

Toradoi came out of her shack.

She wore no chador.

The man who always stood under the hijol tree was not there.

Izzat

Ashapurna Devi

Translated by Rimli Bhattacharya

"Shaughe's about fourteen or fifteen, Boudi," is what she said, but the girl looked at least seventeen or eighteen. And how had Basanti managed to raise such a girl in that basti of theirs? Where had such health come from? And such beauty?

Sumitra could not conceal her surprise. "She is a regular beauty She hardly appears to be your daughter!"

Basanti smiled, a mixture of shame and pride. "That's what they've all been saying ever since she was this little. She takes after her father, see? He was a very handsome man, died of a snakebite. And then the mother-in-law started off at me, as though I had become a snake to harm her son. That kind of hell made me come away to a free life here. Well, no one had seen that man, Boudi. So they tease me and say, You must've stolen a girl from the babus!"

Sumitra smiled slightly and said, "I feel the same, you know. You had been working for me all these days, and I did not even know you had such a daughter."

The pride on Basanti's face faded somewhat. "I used to bring her along with me when she was little, and she helped me quite a bit. But once she was grown up, she just didn't want to leave the house at all. I'll do all your housework, is what she would say, I feel shy to go to the babus' houses. . . . So I told her, Well, if you don't want to go, don't. . . . But there are dangers with such a girl, as I've just told you. If you would be kind enough to give her shelter . . ."

Although Sumitra had said that Basanti had been working for her "all these days," it really had not been that long a time. Her old servant had gone home and that was when Basanti had come to work for four months. Sumitra remembered her as she was polite and neat in her work. But that didn't warrant her coming up with such an absurd proposal as "Keep the girl."

There were a few goondas who had come into the basti and they had made life difficult for Basanti's daughter. The mother had her livelihood to earn and couldn't sit at home all day and guard her daughter. One had to slave the whole day to feed two people, and then there was the rent for the house.

It was just a while ago that God had been kind to her and a job with a fat salary had come Basanti's way. She had to "manage" a rich old lady. Seventy rupees as salary, with meals, oil and soap, and paan-dokta and tea besides. All she had to do was look after the old woman and run errands for her. The old woman was crippled by rheumatism, but she had elegant tastes. Basanti had to soap her during her bath, do up her hair with scented oil, rub her with powder after the oil massage for rheumatism . . . how much could the daughter-in-law do? In any case, they could afford it. That's why they had gone out of their way to keep Basanti at such high wages.

"I was getting along so happily, Boudi," said Basanti. "I would be there by five in the morning and would get back at ten. The girl would wait at other people's homes until I got back. I never had my dinner at the babus' house, I'd bring my share home and it did fine for the two of us. We hardly spent anything. She boiled a little rice for herself in the afternoons. I'd been saving the salary for a few months for her marriage. But, Boudi, the way things change . . ."

Basanti's voice took on a philosophical note. "That man, God, is quite a miser. He just doesn't know how to give with open hands. If he gives with one hand, he snatches away everything with the other. Happiness didn't last for very long. The old woman has started something new these days. She stays awake the whole night and makes people run errands. She'll wake up her sons and her daughters-in-law and tell them, Switch on the lights, switch on the fan. Then she'll say, Give me some water, or Make me a paan. And if you're a little late she starts cursing. Those sons work hard the whole day, running that big business. How are they to bear such demands at night? And now they're after me: We'll pay you ten rupees more, you'd better spend the nights here. If you don't agree, then we'll have to keep someone else. And here I've gone and thrown away my regular washing jobs. And now what am I to do? These rich people can get rid of you whenever they want to."

Not knowing exactly how to respond, Sumitra said, "Quite right."

"But, Boudi, you can't settle it by just saying, Quite right. I've come to your door, now it's all in your hands—you can kill her or keep her."

Sumitra understood Basanti's problem and was sympathetic but she didn't understand why it should be her door, when there were doors all over the country. Basanti must have worked for so many people all these years of her life and she had only worked for Sumitra for a few months. Besides, what about the people she was working for now? What about those people who were willing to pay ten rupees more to keep Basanti during the nights to look after the invalid?

So she told Basanti, "Why don't you take her there with you, since you say it's a huge house that these rich people have. . . . You can keep an eye on your daughter while you watch over the patient."

Basanti beat her forehead and she said in an aggrieved voice, "And have I not said as much to them. I've begged and pleaded. But the babus are very hard. The house is full of servants, they say. And since then, these last two days I've been going around to all the houses I know of, looking for shelter. No one's agreed. All of them come up with different excuses. I've been taking the girl with me. Perhaps the babus will feel kindly if they see her. But . . . "

Sumitra thought to herself, "And that's where you've made a wrong move, my Basantibala. If you hadn't shown them your daughter, somebody may have agreed." Who would agree to keep this fire hazard in their home? Who would give her shelter? And Basanti not being there either? How would it ever work out?

The girl stood in a corner of the veranda wearing a coarsely spun striped sari. And an equally cheap-looking red blouse, probably bought off the pavements. She looked stunning even in these clothes. If you saw her once, you would want to see her again. How beautiful this girl would look if she were well-dressed and lived a life of some comfort. Sumitra decided to give her some of her old saris and blouses and mentally sorted out the precise ones she would give. The georgette with the red flowers was a little worn out in parts, but the color was still very bright. She'd give her that. The blue Bangalore was intact, but it was quite out of fashion now and was lying in the heap of her discarded clothes. That too, she would give. There were also a couple of printed saris faded by repeated trips to the dhobi. And there were innumerable blouses which would fit the girl. In her mind's eye, she dressed up the girl in the red and blue saris. She had once bought some powder manufactured by an unknown company to help out a canvassing sales girl. It was still there, unused. She decided to give that to the girl as well.

She felt pity for the girl and was sorry that such a girl was born a maidservant's daughter and had to rot way in the basti. But some presents would assuage her uneasiness.

Basanti had said, "It's a tiger's cave that we live in, Boudi—a snake pit. That girl's beauty spells doom."

Sumitra was unable to discover any means of protecting her from the tiger and snake, but she was busy spinning out ways of enhancing this doomed beauty. The strange thing was, she could not detect the contradiction in her own thoughts. Her silence encouraged Basanti. "Mounang sammati lakshanam," as they say. Considering Sumitra's silence to be a sigh of her willingness, Basanti eagerly went on, "Then shall I leave her here from today, Boudi? She'll eat your leftovers, and will work as much as she can. If you let her enter the kitchen she'll do all your cooking. And whatever housework you tell her to . . . "

Sumitra became a bit absentminded and said softly, "It's not the work, I already have people to do the work. And there's not much cooking to be done for two people. But I'm wondering. . . . I haven't yet asked your Dadababu . . . "

Basanti realized that she had softened and hastily added, pressing home her advantage, "And what is there to ask Dadababu? Whatever you are, so is Dadababu. In the home, you are queen. You don't have male servants in your house, that's why I've come to you. Please don't say No any more. Please come back either today or tomorrow and hand her over with her clothes. Joyi, come here and take the dust off your Maima's feet. You're going to live here. You'll do everything as your Maima says, help her out in every way. Until you get married and go off to your in-laws, this house of your Maima's is going to be your home."

Sumitra, however, hesitated a bit. "But, I was saying, is she going to like being . . . "

"No more buts, Boudi," Basanti continued in an emotional voice. "How can she not like being here with a person such as you? What all you say! Living there in the jaws of Yama, the girl has quite shriveled up. Those haramzada boys, whether you look or not, they'll whistle at her, sing obscene songs, make rude gestures, push past her every time she goes to the pump to fetch water. And as for the other things, it would be sinful to even talk about them." Basanti lowered her voice and then proceeded to tell her about these "sinful" episodes.

Sumitra was shocked.

Basanti put her anchal to her eyes and said, "Why do you think I've been pleading with you. We're poor people who wash dishes to earn our living. But for us women, isn't there a question of izzat too? You are educated people with so much learning. You understand it all. It's up to you now to keep her izzat."

Sumitra's heart began to beat wildly. There were tigers waiting to pounce on that beautiful girl. If she wanted to, she could save her. A hooded snake hissed over that girl's head, and if Sumitra showed a little kindness she could protect her. Wasn't she going to do even that much? Would it really be so difficult for her if a poor girl was given shelter in a corner of her house?

A frantic mother's heart wanted to entrust Sumitra with the responsibility of safeguarding the izzat of her vulnerable young girl. Was Sumitra going to ignore that? The plea was being laid at the door of her conscience and was she going to shut that door? Was she going to say, "You take care of your daughter's izzat. Why should you try to dump your responsibility on me?" But she could not say that and said the only thing she could.

Overjoyed, Basanti began to cry. Now there was no stopping her. She could not be dissuaded from falling at Sumitra's feet. And, as she rubbed that hand on her own head and her face, she said, "I knew you would be kind. You are Bhagawati herself. All the many houses I've been to, they just wouldn't listen to what I had to say."

Then, she added with some embarrassment, "So, let me keep her here for now, Boudi, and go tell them at the big house. I'll fetch her at night. Tonight, mother and daughter, we'll eat together and I'll bring her over in the morning with her sari and blouse."

Sumitra smiled and thought, "I shall not let your daughter lack for clothes."

Sumitra then opened her almirah and sat down to sort through her old clothes. Basanti was going to be amazed when she came next time to see her daughter. The girl was not just beautiful, there was something pleasing and respectable about the expression on her face. Sumitra was going to give her a new life. She was going to teach her to read and write. Sumitra began to think on those lines, unmindful of her own position.

But Mohitosh was quite aware of Sumitra's position. So he cried out in violent objection, "What do you mean you've given her your word? You didn't even think it was necessary to ask me once?"

"She begged me . . . " Sumitra replied in some confusion.

"And why wouldn't she? They're ready to lick the dust off your feet if it means getting the job done. That doesn't mean that you have to take on such a responsibility. Impossible!"

"The girl can't survive at their basti anymore," said Sumitra with some force. "She can't because she is a good, respectable girl. If she was bad, she would've been ruined a long time ago in that environment. Are we to throw a girl like this to the wolves?"

"There are all sorts of things happening in the world," said Mohitosh. "Are you capable of being responsible for everyone?"

"If not for everyone, at least for one person."

"Forget those poetic sentiments!" retorted Mohitosh, heatedly. "You must act after the proper consideration. I've seen the girl. A girl like that can't remain good in such low-class surroundings."

Sumitra replied, her face bright red, "Whatever they may be, there is no reason for you to talk like a lower-class person. If that is indeed the case, then why should her mother come to me, so upset and so anxious?"

"They are up to all kinds of tricks."

"What sort of trick can you be thinking of?" asked Sumitra in a low voice. "If you had heard everything you wouldn't have been able to say No either. Some scoundrels have started plaguing her so much that she's told her mother, One day Ma, you'll come back home to find me hanging from the beam."

"But why does the mother need to take up that job?"

"Look, we all need money. They need it even more. The poor thing has been thinking about her daughter's marriage."

Mohitosh said scornfully, "How many thousands do you need for a maid-servant's daughter's wedding?"

Sumitra was hurt and could not bear his contempt for the poor. Her voice hardened. "Let's forget all that for a minute. Do you think that even if she sits there guarding her daughter, she will be able to do so? She's quite helpless. They'll probably snatch her away before her very eyes."

But Mohitosh retorted sarcastically, "I see they've come up with a lot of stories to win over their Boudi. Don't talk to me about them—they can really cook up stories. She's made up this rigmarole to foist her daughter on you! What are you going to do if she now calls the police and tells them that the babus have forcibly taken away her daughter?"

Sumitra was obliged to sit down. "I find that they are not the only ones capable of cooking up stories. How did you even think of such a thing?"

"Why shouldn't I? I don't go around looking at the world through rose-tinted glasses like you do! Do you know about the kind of scams that go on in a place like Calcutta? Are you aware at all how regularly these kind of cases come up? You'll find that that very same girl will strip off your mask of respectability and say, Yes, the babus had brought me along to work for them, and now they won't let me go. . . . If they want, they can even trump up a scandalous charge against me."

"And what is she to get out of it?" Sumitra's voice was as hard as stone.

"Anyone would think that you've just been born. Don't you know what she's going to get out of it? Squeeze money out of us. Those goondas she mentioned, quite possibly they're her accomplices. They'll come over to our house to gherao and abuse us. It's unthinkable. Get rid of her right away. You said something about her coming over at night. Well, you can tell her then, it's not going to work. Dadababu hasn't agreed."

Sumitra looked at him steadily. "This means I have to tell this maidservant that I have no say in this household."

Mohitosh said with utter disregard for her words, "And what a person before whom your prestige is going to be shattered! Keep your poetry aside and try to be a little practical. Supposing that all I've told you actually happens, what will you do then?"

"And supposing nothing of that sort happens. Supposing that by some strange chance that maidservant is actually telling the truth?"

"Well, she should sort out her own daughter's problems. Why can't she talk to all the people in the basti?"

"Then you think that if she were to tell all the people in the basti they would take the responsibility of protecting her izzat?"

Mohitosh replied with some enthusiasm, "And why shouldn't they? Not everyone is a bad sort. A lot of respectable types live there with their families. If they all come together it won't take long to silence those goondas."

"Then you believe that those basti people have more humanity than you? And more power?"

"Go on, say what you like," said Mohitosh. "But I'm not going to agree to let your Basantibala's daughter stay here. Even if we assume it is not a trap, that girl herself is quite capable of causing a scandal in our home."

A faint and somewhat twisted smile played around Sumitra's lips. "With whom? We have no male servants in the house."

Mohitosh laughed heartily "Well, perhaps with the master. With her kind of stunning looks!"

Sumitra said in a low voice, "That's all the more reason, isn't it, why we should in fact keep her? To find out what is brass and what is gold."

"Stop talking nonsense!" he retorted angrily. "When her mother comes you had better tell her that there's no question of shelter here."

"You can do the telling."

"I? Why should it be me? I don't talk to these maidservant types of yours. You will tell her whatever has to be said."

"I can't. I've given her my word."

"If you go around giving your word without considering your position, you are bound to be in an uncomfortable situation," said Mohitosh angrily "A maidservant comes, tells you a load of rubbish, and gets you to make her some kind of a promise, and now so much talk of being bound by it! All right, if you can't tell her, I shall."

And so he did.

Sumitra could hear them from her room. She heard Basanti's tearful voice pleading, "Dadababu, please call Boudi, just once. We had agreed and I went to tell the people in the big house . . . "

Mohitosh's voice was hard. "Boudi has a headache. She's lying down."

"Let me go to the door then, Dadababu. I'll tell her, Boudi, don't dash my hopes . . . "

"No! No! She mustn't be disturbed. She's very unwell and can't even lift her head."

Basanti cried some more and at that moment Sumitra heard a voice filled with anguish. "That's enough, Ma. Come away. There's no need to cry and call on Boudi. It's clear who has the last word in this house. You're not to fall at their feet, thinking of your daughter's izzat. The babus don't care about the izzat of a low-class girl. All right. If we are low-down people, we'll have to settle for a low-down life. If we have to go to the dogs then that's what we'll do."

Sumitra heard two pairs of feet pounding down the stairs, and then . . . silence.

Mohitosh entered the room and demanded, "Did you hear them talk? And that's the girl you thought was civilized. Respectable! Huh!"

Sumitra could not reply. She truly could not lift her head. It felt as if it was being torn apart because she did not have the power to look after a young woman's izzat.

But which young woman's?

JUSTICE

Urmila Pawar
Translated by Asha Damle

After fifteen long years I decided to visit my native village. To tell you the truth, I didn't really want to. Since my mother died, I have had no close family there. Besides, the place is so awkwardly situated. It is four miles from the nearest town, across a lagoon, and deep inside a gorge with all those sheer slopes all around it. To walk all the way is next to impossible. I don't like the villagers either; their manners, their diction is so idiotic. No common sense at all!

Here in Bombay I practice law. I am doing well. I live with my family in a nice flat with all the modern gadgets one could possibly have. I don't care any more for that dilapidated old house where my father lived or for the two-odd acres of ancestral land. There's no way I will ever go back and live there. So I decided to return to sell the piece of land, and the house as well.

I reached the place at night, and all I could see in the feeble light of a hurricane lamp was the spot where I stepped. Now in the early morning light, I was pleasantly surprised to see a luscious green thicket of banana trees. The bananas that clung together looked like lively newborn babies, clasping their hands in greeting to the new world. Little streams had been channeled off the main well. The running water gurgled, and tickled my bare feet. I felt proud of Kushaba. I had asked him to cultivate the land around the house, and through his hard work he had turned it into a gold mine. The thought that I had come to snatch all this away from Kushaba made me feel uncomfortable. But what else could I do?

I was going to sell my land to the Village Elder. We had been in touch with each other, sorting out matters. I had informed Kushaba as well, by letter. I was expecting the Village Elder to come and see me. Vishnu—my neighbor, the teacher—and I, were sitting on the veranda. While waiting, we chatted about the price of land and about inflation in general.

I heard footsteps and turned around. Old Kushaba was standing at the door and, a few steps behind him, was a young woman. Kushaba was very old now, his head was shaking and there was sadness written all over his wrinkled face. Forcing a smile, he greeted me.

"Come in, Kushaba, come in, and tell us . . . how are you?"

"By the grace of God, and your lordship, sir, I am fine."

The words came out, steeped in insufferable pain. That was natural.

Kushaba signaled the young woman to come forward. She stepped ahead, put down the basket she was carrying and stood there humbly. The fresh, plump ripe bananas looked so tempting.

"You shouldn't have . . . " I said as I looked at the woman.

She was strong and healthy and voluptuous. Even a man of fifty like me would be tempted to steal a touch if she was in a crowd. Fair of face, she was quite tanned by the hot sun. Her face tapered at the chin. Tapering chins are unlucky they say. I realized suddenly that she was not wearing the red mark of a married woman on her forehead. She was a widow!

"Well, who is she, I mean . . . "

"She is my daughter-in-law, sir." The old man fumbled. His head began to shake.

"She is his only son's wife, Paru. Five years back her husband was drowned in the lagoon." Vishnu stated the facts in his uncouth manner. It was embarrassing to hear him state it in his crude manner in front of Paru and her father-in-law. "Now, the old man has no one else to help him out . . . " I felt pity.

I made Kushaba sit near me and tried to explain why I had to sell the land. I said I would ask the Village Elder to pay an additional one thousand rupees for the banana orchard. And all this money I said I'd give to Kushaba. Even then his face did not light up. He wanted to say something to me. My business sense prompted me to say no more. What if he were to make an unreasonable demand? Then perhaps the Village Elder wouldn't accept the bargain and I would be at a loss, not knowing how to finalize the sale.

"May I take your leave, sir?" Kushaba got up. His mind was not at ease. Paru had already walked away ahead of him.

Vishnu scoffed at Kushaba as he left. "See the simple, innocent demeanor of the daughter-in-law? But beneath that garb, things are not what they seem."

"What do you mean? I don't understand."

My ignorance lent gusto to Vishnu's narration. I was flabbergasted by what he said.

Paru was good looking. I had noticed she looked intelligent and capable. Her manners were polite and non-interfering. She had seemed quiet, collected. Her husband had died right after their marriage. Since then, she had literally wasted away her youth. She sweated and toiled on my two acres of land and had raised this beautiful orchard. She carried the fruit on her head to the market in the town, walking all the way on the unmade stretch of four miles to the neighboring town. She and her father-in-law lived on her labor. The good woman was now sixteen weeks pregnant. Nobody knew who the father was, but they had a hunch. They suspected young Shantanu. The boy was from a well-to-do family, and was a postgraduate student. Every day he cycled to the university college in the neighboring town. Paru's time to go to the market often coincided with his. On these premises, Vishnu and the village folk built their theory that . . .

Vishnu's narration was vivid, as if he had actually witnessed everything. Some people do take an interest in gossiping—almost as if it were food for their brain. Vishnu was such a person.

I was annoyed at his precocious remarks.

"Are you suggesting that you saw both of them necking and kissing?"

"Maybe once or twice, chatting away merrily."

"The rest is your fabrication! This won't stand up in a court of law! Where's the evidence, the eyewitnesses?"

This time Vishnu ridiculed me. "What a thing to say! Do you mean to say a man and a woman copulate in the sight of others? Even married couples who derive sanctions from the priest and God do not mate in front of everybody . . . "

Vishnu was in a triumphant mood as he was able to contradict me.

Just then, the Village Elder entered and our talk ended.

"Good morning, sir," I said briskly. "I've been waiting for you. We must try and finish the deal today. I have to go back to my job in the court, you know."

"Whatever you say, but how can I help it? All these nasty, dirty matters in the village crop up and I am helpless!"

"What nasty matters?" I pleaded innocent.

"This Kushaba's silly daughter-in-law, what an idiot of a woman!"

Now he told me the whole story in his words. I noticed that his story was very similar to Vishnu's.

"I wonder how these things happen?" I said. "She is a young widow . . . "

"Never imagined her to be like this." The Village Elder raised his stiff upper lip.

"Well, well, don't you know:

> A child knows not
> An old man cannot
> If a youth does not, life is but a naught!"

Vishnu recited his stanza rather loudly and both of them laughed aloud.

To me, such things were not new. Sometimes they were settled out of court, sometimes the guilty received a sentence. More often than not, the culprit found a loophole in the law and escaped.

"Sir," said the Village Elder, "I request you. Let us postpone this sale for a while. I am not able to concentrate on it right now."

I stared at him. Maybe, maybe he was the culprit. Even an old man was still capable of such an act. I had observed Vishnu closely but he only seemed talkative. He had no guts for such adventures. He only enjoyed what others did.

"Yes, sir, you look really worried." My gaze pierced him.

"Well, I can tell you, I am. And then, there is that Nagya, breathing down my neck!"

"Who is that?"

"Nagya is Paru's brother. He has come from Bombay. He is a layabout from Worli, a goonda. In fact, I invited him. I wanted him to know what his sister was like. Instead, he has trapped me. He is asking for justice. Give justice to my sister, otherwise I will kill everybody concerned, he says. He is quite capable of killing a few in cold blood."

"Is it true that Paru has accused Shantanu?"

"No, not a word from her yet. Nagya gave Paru a good hiding to get the truth out of her."

"Then . . ."

"She says she will make her statement at the meeting tonight!"

"There's to be real drama, then!" Vishnu was very excited.

I ignored him and asked, "Suppose she accuses Shantanu. Will you force him to marry her?"

"Of course, I will have to. I had hoped to fine Shantanu heavily for causing dishonor but I don't think Nagya will accept such a deal." The old man started scratching his gray hair.

"Listen, sir, now that you are here, you be the judge. People will listen to you and there will be no more trouble."

"That's nonsense. You village folk must decide. This is not a court of law. You can decide on things the way you want to. You don't have to uphold the formal law." I tried to get out of it. I didn't want to involve myself with these villagers. I had nothing to do with them.

I was enjoying my siesta in the veranda that afternoon. My thoughts hovered over Paru's affair as if she were my client.

"Sir!"

"Who is it?"

I lifted my head. There was another woman. I guessed she was Shantanu's mother judging from her demeanor, and I was right.

"Come in, sit down," I got up and said coldly.

"Sir, I am Shantanu's mother . . . " and, taking a few quick breaths, she continued, "Sir, you know it all . . . "

"Yes, yes. I know that your son is the culprit." I sounded like a lawyer.

Tears welled up in her eyes as she heard me. Choking on her breath, she blurted out, "Sir, save my son, sir!"

"How can I? And that girl Paru, what about her?" My voice had a rasping tone.

On hearing Paru's name, Shantanu's mother pounced on me like a tigress. She cursed Paru profusely. She blamed her for everything. She even accused her of deliberate slander.

I let her speak. I let her shout. At least it purged her mind of all the rage. Then I tried to console her. "I can understand your rage but still, you should see Paru and make her understand."

"She came to our house, to see Shantanu," Shantanu's mother said, crestfallen.

"Well, then?"

"She didn't say a lot. She said that she had to think of her future. She needed someone in her lonely life."

"Then you should have offered her something—some gold, some land."

"She is not prepared to listen, the fool that she is."

Why should she? She was going to earn a husband and all his wealth, why should she be happy with whatever you condescend to offer, I thought.

One thing was clear. Paru was involved with Shantanu and she was exploiting the situation cleverly. She knew she couldn't live on my land any more, so she was trying to provide for her future. She had got her goonda brother to threaten Shantanu. She had trapped Shantanu completely. I had nothing but praise for this unlettered village woman. Even a smart, educated, city-bred woman would not dare to manipulate the situation so adroitly.

I consoled Shantanu's mother, somehow. What I really felt was pity for that boy, Shantanu. He was so young. He had succumbed to a moment of intense temptation. Was he to suffer for that all his life? Soon he would get his postgraduate degree. He must have dreams of marrying someone as well educated as himself. But one moment of devilish temptation had set him on a ruinous path, had tagged him to this uneducated village girl.

I just couldn't make up my mind. Okay, so if he had been my son I would have been angry with him. I would have raved and ranted, but would I not have tried to save him? Should I ask Shantanu to see me? Should I advise him to deny the whole affair and push her away? Was there any other loophole I could think of?

But then, another moment, and my mind moved on to a more vexing problem. What if Paru were my daughter? What would I have done? Would I not have agreed with her and supported the stand she had taken? It was her life . . .

I decided finally that this was not my headache. I'd have a quiet read and relax and leave the matter to the village council. But the Village Elder came and dragged me to the meeting.

The meeting was held in the marquee in front of the village temple. There were around twelve chairs for the dignitaries set against the temple steps and facing the audience. There were other Elders: the sheriff, the revenue collector and the school headmaster. There was only one table in front of the row of chairs. The audience was divided along the center into two groups, men on one side, women on the other. Anxiety, curiosity, lit up their faces. They could not wait to watch the drama that was to unfold. They all talked in agitated whispers. You could feel the rawness of their emotions.

The Village Elder wanted me to join him, but I preferred to sit with the audience. Vishnu noticed me and came and sat next to me. Because of him, I could put names to many of the faces.

"And that one, sir, the one sitting behind the pillar in a blue shirt, that is Shantanu."

I turned to observe him. He was some ten feet away from us. He seemed quite well built and healthy but his shoulders drooped and his head fell on his chest, like a person who's been defeated in a wrestling match. I had not expected him to be there. Nagya must have bullied him into coming.

I turned my gaze towards the womenfolk. There was Shantanu's mother, her head covered by her sari, scarf-like. She looked so pitiful. The sight of the mother and the son sent fear creeping down my spine.

Suddenly, everyone was quiet. Vishnu nudged me. "Sir, look, there's Nagya."

I looked to the front. Nagya was standing near the table. He wasn't a well built man, but with his chin up, chest forward and his couldn't-care-less attitude, he inspired a certain fearful respect for himself in people's minds. I know that all goondas have this trait. They have nothing to lose, and always spot the weak points and exploit them. Nagya must have drunk a big measure of country wine. His red eyes glowered and with intimidating steps he came and plonked himself on a chair. Marigolds peeped out from a bag he was holding.

"What are the garlands for?" I asked Vishnu.

"Maybe for the wedding!" Vishnu's eyes lit up.

I thought of them as wreaths for Shantanu's coffin.

The meeting started as soon as Nagya was seated. The Village Elder stood up. Without much ado he came straight to the point. "Everyone knows that

Kushaba Hubha Surve, a resident of our village, has a daughter-in-law, Parvati. She has been a widow for the last five years. The point is that the widow is now sixteen weeks pregnant. The village wants an explanation. I summon Parvati to come forward, face the gathering and answer the questions we ask."

He looked at the womenfolk and signaled to two of them. The women got up, went behind the temple and fetched Paru.

Everyone's gaze was now fixed on Paru, all arrows were ready to shoot. Paru was wearing a nine-yard sari, fully covering her body. She had the end of the sari pulled over her head. She stood motionless in front of Nagya.

The oldest man in the village, Subhanrao, stood up. He observed her from top to toe and asked the first question. "What is your name?"

"Parvati Bapu Surve." Paru's tone was clear, with no trace of fear.

"Age?"

"Twenty-seven."

"Means of livelihood?"

"I work in the orchard, sell the fruit, do any other odd jobs."

This continued for a while. She answered every question directly and promptly.

Subhanrao now came to the point.

"Are you pregnant?"

"Yes."

"How many weeks is it?"

"Sixteen." There was no change in her tone.

"Who is the father? Speak. Tell us his name."

"I . . . I . . . I don't know."

Nagya stood up and thundered, "Paru! Tell the truth!"

People tittered.

"What? Do you mean to say you don't know his name, the name of the person with whom. . . ?" probed Subhanrao.

"No. I really don't know, because . . .

"Because what?"

"Because I was raped."

"What are you talking about, Paru?" Nagya held Paru's hand in a tight grip.

"But who did it? Who was he?" Subhanrao, who was asking the questions, fumbled. He was tense.

"I don't know. I didn't see." Paru was calm once more.

"Don't you try to hide anything! Come out with whatever is the truth." Nagya was losing his hold. He seemed to want to give her a good hiding.

"I am telling you the truth. Please listen. I demand justice."

Paru's words came out clearly.

"Everyone knows that I go to the town to sell the bananas I grow. Our village is awkwardly situated. The road is very lonely, there's hardly anybody to walk with." She stopped to catch her breath. "I was going to the market as usual. The basket I was carrying on my head was heavy with fruit. I was trying to walk fast. Suddenly, someone from behind pounced on me. I fell down heavily along with my basket. A piece of cloth was thrown on my face. It covered my mouth and nose forcibly. Before I could say anything, I lost consciousness. When I came to, I realized I had been raped."

No smart, city-bred, educated lady could have delivered in such a telling voice her pleading speech from the stand of an accused person. Paru did it.

People stood speechless when they heard her. Nobody knew what to say. Only the Village Elder, glowering at her, raised his voice and said, "Why didn't you say so before?"

"Yes, why didn't you? Why didn't you?" People agreed with him.

"What would you have done?" Paru's question was loud and clear.

Everyone was nonplussed. Indeed! What could they have done? Whom would they have arrested?

"What about that sin, that child growing inside you?" an old man asked.

Paru stood in front of the crowd, her sturdy hands placed squarely on her stomach. "I want my baby. He is mine. I will raise him. I will look after him."

"No, no. That's an illegitimate child. We won't let you." The revenue collector joined in for the first time.

"Why not? I am a woman. I have feelings. I have a heart. Every woman hopes to be a mother one day. I feel the same way. Never mind who the father is, I am the mother. I need someone. I am a widow. I will have nobody when I grow old. Is there anyone else amongst you who would come forward and give me the support I need?"

Paru held them in a trance as she threw her question at them.

Nobody had an answer. Nobody came forward. I glanced at Shantanu stealthily. He held his chin up, proud of her, his eyes full of gratitude, his gaze concentrated on her. I was moved, too.

Next day, the Village Elder came to see me with all the documents for the sale of my land and house. I was ready and waiting.

"Come on, let us get on with the job you came for," he said.

"Excuse me," I said. "I have changed my mind. I don't want to sell my land." The Village Elder looked askance.

Quite proud of myself and of what I was doing, I said, "Would you have me make my daughter homeless?"

A Kind of Love Story

Mrinal Pande
Translated by the author

Madhusudan Babu put the razor on the table and began to rub his chin with a lump of alum. The razor had a sharp edge that nicked the skin easily, drawing blood. Made in Germany, it said on the cracked handle. It was only in Germany that they produced goods that could be used for several generations, Madhusudan Babu thought, as he carefully rinsed the razor under the tap. He gently patted the razor's edge with his towel, and, just as carefully folded it and put it away in an old box.

These days they can't make anything properly, can they? Take, for example, a harmonium. What copper reeds and scales they fixed them with in those days, and what perfect tuning the instruments had! You only had to lay a finger on a key and the note rang out loud and clear, with not a hair's breadth of difference in the shrutis. Not like the modern ones that you have to work like an ironsmith's bellows. And such cheap monstrosities too, these—all colored plastic and shiny, as though the keyboard were a harlot's skirt! Why, even inside, the reeds are just glued together anyhow. Come monsoon, and they all come unstuck and your instrument is khallas for good!

It is the same with the tanpuras. Earlier they had inlay work on the body with real ivory and the bridge that supported the strings was ivory too, sandpapered to a delicate finish, so that as you strummed the strings, they resonated with the deep sustained sounds of monsoon clouds in summer. These days they've begun using the same cheap plastic for the bridge and the same ghastly glue for the tanpura as well. What is worse, the tomba shell will be misshapen and the tuning pegs mismatched. Madhusudan Babu didn't feel like even touching such instruments.

With a grimace, he replaced the little lump of alum in the cloth bag where it had been housed for two decades, and got up to put everything away.

Actually, this age suffers from a poverty of the soul, no? Not only things but also the hearts of men have deteriorated. In those days young musicians nearly killed themselves practicing, doing riyaz before the sun rose, singing the same note over and over again for hours together, learning those intricate Merukhand paltas by rote. Who wants to go through all that now? Now you mug up four or five alankaras, learn the names of a few rare raags, pick up a few gestures and expressions that draw applause on stage and, after a mere year's taleem, you may call yourself a gharana singer. Such charlatans will sing Raag Darbari Kanhara like the Jaunpuri, and the foolish listeners will go into ecstasies! To tell the truth, it was these asinine listeners who created such semi-musicians. A music festival, and hordes of them will descend as though it were a charitable feast. Arre! Can one even ask, "What do you know, son?"

His late ustad used to say that a little knowledge was a most dangerous thing. May his soul rest in peace. Wah! How his ustad's face glowed, what an air of confidence his person had. Truly, his music was a siddhi, a spiritual accomplishment. When he sang Raag Shri and touched the flat rishabha, it felt as though a dagger had pierced right through your heart! It was said that to acquire this power, his ustad had sat meditating in a dark cave for seven years under the guidance of a Kanphatia Baba. He had acquired such rare mastery over his breathing processes that his voice swam gracefully through three octaves like a fish swimming in divine waters. To hear him sing Raag Todi was to have your heart melt like a lump of butter.

The nasal tones of the teacher of the neighborhood Sangeet Mahavidyalaya wafted in through Madhusudan Babu's window. *Piya ki Najariya* . . . sang the teacher in a dull monotone. Word by word, note by note, the ass was dismembering the lovely evening raag, Yaman. Madhusudan Babu banged his window shut, locked up the house, and slowly began to descend the staircase. Arthritis had started to bother him. He had to hold on to the walls as he climbed down, and many years had passed since he had sat on the floor to practice.

What a long race this life was! You ran and ran endlessly till the call came from above. His parents had left him an orphan as a child. Then had followed a bleak spell of dire poverty when he lived with his mother's brother and somehow managed to finish his Entrance Classes. Finally, he managed a job in a transport company. The future stood before him with an open mouth and he had no dreams. It was then that he heard his ustad sing a mehfil, and realized in a flash that he had become a slave of those pure notes. So, all day long he worked at the transport company and in the evenings, he went and served at the ustad's feet. For twenty seven years, till the day the ustad breathed his last. The ustad was like a father to him. Wasn't his soul reborn because of the ustad, recharged with the nectar of those musical notes? "Arre, Madhusudan," he would say, "learn this, you son of an ass! Once I die, the pure notes shall die, too."

That is what happened. As soon as the ustad died, his three wives gathered their children and left. Madhusudan Babu was left behind with the priceless collection of musical instruments, to buy which his ustad had often gone without meals—the harmonium with real German reeds and ivory keys, the tanpura from Meeraj with its base made of imported African pumpkin, and a pair of rare tabla drums from Pune that tinkled to the touch.

Now the tanpura stands in a corner for months on end, all wrapped up in its cover. Each Guru Poornima, on the day of the full moon, Madhusudan Babu cleans and polishes these instruments and remembers his guru. Otherwise, the tanpura and the tabla lie idle. The harmonium he plays sometimes, placing it on a table, so he doesn't have to bend. Though his fingers no longer retain their old touch, the harmonium is shipshape. Not a single key plays out of tune. The boys from the music school across the road had once come to ask him if they could borrow his harmonium for Saraswati Puja. He'd growled and chased them away. Are music instruments gas lanterns that you dare borrow them for a community event? In any case, he had never liked to beg for or share things. Neither a borrower nor a lender be, his ustad had often said. Madhusudan Babu cleared his throat and spat on the roadside. No, he suffered no guilt, though among the neighbors he was known as an ill-tempered old grouch. He didn't care one way or another.

Keeping his lean body straight, Madhusudan Babu turned right and reached the market. He picked up a bunch of radish, a quarter kilo of gourd, one cake of Chandani soap and a packet of Isabgol husk. He then put the purse in his pocket, changed the now heavy bag from one hand to the other, and retraced his steps.

A crowd of holidaying schoolchildren was darting across the road in hot pursuit of falling kites. They did not care for the traffic lights or the hooting vehicles going up and down. Madhusudan Babu grimaced and crossed over to the other side of the road. The world would be a veritable heaven if only women and children were not in it. All the woes of the world one could lay at their feet, no? He thought of the three wives his ustad had had, and their intrigues and yelling and the unearthly din created by their innumerable children. His ustad sat quiet and unruffled in the middle of that hell, like a lotus flower in a field of mud. The ustad and his music were untouched by the ugliness around. But how long could his body have coped with poverty? He died, his lungs eaten up by tuberculosis. Who was there to get him the medicines and milk and fruits that he needed in order to survive? True, Madhusudan Babu had done what little he could, but his salary was small. Like one pomegranate and a hundred sick people, it disappeared in no time. At the end, his ustad's lungs—which at one time had had the power to fuel taans that lasted for four rounds of taal—wheezed and begged for each small breath.

This was when Madhusudan Babu decided not to have a family himself. His small job gave him enough to live on and, after retirement, it brought him a pension which was quite adequate. He was very happy with no daughter to marry off, no son to be employed and no wife to cringe before.

Once home, Madhusudan Babu put the bag down and changed his clothes. In his kitchen, with its containers all neatly labeled and arranged in rows, he lit the stove, put the kettle on, and started cutting vegetables for his evening meal of khichri and vegetables. No spicy pickles and chutneys for him, no thank you! He would finish off his wholesome dinner with his tonic, Chyavanprash, and his daily glass of milk.

The kettle had come to the boil. Madhusudan Babu brewed himself a good cup of tea, put the khichri to cook and went and sat near the window.

The evening music classes in the school across the road were apparently over, and a cluster of girls had come out nudging each other and giggling. They stood chirping around a trolley that sold spicy chat, wasting their fathers' and brothers' hard-earned money on despicable spicy food.

Madhusudan Babu got up to stir his khichri. It was his opinion that women must be quiet and dignified and speak only when spoken to. But modern parents allowed anything, they even allowed girls to wear trousers these days. Shiva, Shiva!

With a violent bang Madhusudan Babu put the pot down, and set the vegetables to simmer. These neighing fillies will learn music? Hunh! The poet Kabirdas was dead right when he said that even a woman's shadow falling on a snake can blind it—what to say of those that keep the company of women. Praise be to his ustad who warned him off in time.

Dusk was setting in. Madhusudan Babu first lit a lamp before the gods, then an incense stick, and bowed his head in prayer before a picture of Hanuman, the celibate monkey god.

The door rattled. Then a timid knock was heard.

Madhusudan Babu was a little surprised. Who could it be? No one visited him any more. Maybe some mischievous child, passing by? The knock came again. This time it was loud and clear.

Irritated, he moved the latch and behind the half-open door his slender body stood stiff as a whip, ready to lash out at the unwelcome intruder. His eyes glittered with a black rage at the man with graying hair who stood at the threshold.

"I am sorry, are you Shri Madhusudan Sharma?"

"Yes, I am. So?"

"Ji, actually it is like this. I have an old harmonium that belonged to my father . . . "

"So?" Madhusudan Babu began to pick his teeth rudely.

The man looked a little taken aback. "Ji, actually some of the keys tend to get stuck. I'm new to this town and the music school across the road is closed. So they . . . so someone told me you knew a lot about musical instruments. I thought perhaps you could tell me of a reliable shop that repairs them."

"Who told you?" Madhusudan Babu's thick brows were knitted together, his voice came out as a growl.

"Well, some people in the school premises. You see, our harmonium is an old one. It was made in Germany, and I don't want to hand it to just anyone for repairs."

"Hmm."

He stared at the visitor for a few seconds.

"All right. I'll have a look at it. Do you live close by?"

"Yes. I'm sorry for the trouble."

"You'll have to wait for five minutes." Madhusudan Babu gestured the visitor to sit down and removed his shirt from the peg on the wall. "So, you are fond of music?"

"Well, actually, a little. But my father knew quite a lot about it. I've just gathered a few drops of knowledge from him."

Madhusudan Babu approved of this modesty of tone. "Whom did your father receive his taleem from?" he asked, as he stirred the vegetables.

The name that the visitor uttered took him by surprise. A man who had been groomed by an ustad like that! Well, the food could wait. He put the pot down, turned off the stove, and put on his slippers. "Let us go."

The man's house was indeed close by. On the way the visitor told him his name was Damodar Pandeya. His music-loving father had died a year ago. He now lived with his aged mother and a widowed sister, who used to teach in the neighboring town but had resigned her job to nurse their mother. He worked in a bank.

The house, though small, was spotlessly clean. From the curtains to the covers on the cushions, everything was old and worn out, but scrupulously clean and neatly arranged.

Madhusudan Babu took off his slippers outside and went in and sat on the white sheet upon the floor. Damodar went into the next room. Some faint voices arose inside, then Damodar came out with the harmonium. He was panting a little with the effort, but placed the instrument very gently in front of Madhusudan Babu, as though before an idol of a deity.

Madhusudan Babu was pleased to note that the harmonium was neatly protected from dust with a soft quilted cover. Good maintenance of instruments always denoted a genuine devotion to music, his ustad used to say. Then, as he removed the cover, his eyes were dazzled by the sheer beauty of the gem that lay underneath. Aha, what unmatched craftsmanship! The body was genuine rosewood, the keys real ivory and, as he touched the keys, mellifluous notes rang out.

"Wah!" he said, as he ran his fingers over the keys. "This is a really good instrument."

Damodar's pale face lit up with a slow smile. "We have never changed the air-fitting, nor ever tuned the scales."

Madhusudan Babu nodded his head in appreciation. Then he got busy assessing the problem. "Do you have a small file at home? I will also need some sandpaper? And maybe some machine oil as well?" he asked gently.

As he expected, everything was available, a little worn with use, but well maintained and clean. While he was bent over the instrument, a young woman entered the room with a tray bearing tea in two well-scrubbed tumblers. She was introduced to him as Damodar's sister Damayanti. Her face was oval and her skin wheat-colored. Her clothes were old fashioned but not fussy, and were draped neatly. Her entire person had the stamp of clean, disciplined living. She acknowledged the introduction with a smile which was just right.

"Khush raho," Madhusudan Babu said, with genuine warmth.

There was nothing seriously wrong with the instrument. Some of the keys stuck a bit due to disuse. This he set right in a matter of minutes.

He ran his fingers expertly over the keyboard again. Notes rained down effortlessly.

"Wah!" the brother and sister said in unison.

Before anyone realized, it was ten o'clock. Damodar, like Madhusudan Babu himself, turned out to be a veritable mine of information about old raags and compositions, ustads and gharanas. He did not have a musical voice, so his father had not taught him to sing, but he had heard much good music, that was for sure. The three sat till late, discussing music. Madhusudan Babu sang a few old compositions for them. His throat was not at its best, his breath too showed signs of age and fatigue, but any good listener could trace in it the golden vestiges of sound training. As Damodar showered "Wah, Wahs" on him, Damayanti moved her head from side to side in demure appreciation.

Madhusudan Babu suddenly found that the frozen sea of music within his heart had begun to roar and heave. He could, all of a sudden, recall compositions that he didn't even remember he'd learned.

Damayanti had to go in to check on their mother several times, but she did it so quietly, so gently, that it didn't jar. He appreciated that.

When Madhusudan Babu finally got up to leave, Damayanti said hesitatingly that her mother insisted that he eat with them before he left.

The meal was just as he liked it, delicately seasoned and light and served neatly. The old mother lay on a bed in the next room from where she gently begged him to eat more, urging the daughter to serve him all those homemade pickles and jams. "The candied fruits are good for the brain, Bhaiji," the old lady said. "It'll do an artist such as you good."

Madhusudan Babu was a changed man as he walked back. He became a daily visitor to the house, and the house in turn hugged him close as though he were a long lost member.

Slowly, several nameless shoots began to sprout in the bleak desert that was Madhusudan Babu's life. At night, as he laid his head upon the pillow, old forgotten compositions and tunes would ring in his ears. As he lay listening to this music within, Damayanti's gentle voice would waft in, imploring him to eat more, asking him if the curd was not too sour. Shiva! Shiva! Shiva! The harder he tried to focus his thoughts on music and Lord Shiva, the more, like naughty calves that have broken their ropes, they would go galloping towards the other house.

Damayanti! Damayanti! The very name acquired a divine glow in his thoughts. The little obstinate chin, those gentle curves of her muscular arms as she rolled out his chapattis, the glow of the fire upon her cheeks. Damayanti! Damayanti! In his room, Madhusudan Babu would often sit up till late, singing old thumris

O beloved, do not leave me,
I shall take fright if you do!

His heart, which was once closed tight like a narrow and dingy room, now seemed lit up and caressed by gentle breezes. When he asked his barber to shape his sideburns carefully one morning, the poor man gaped at him. Madhusudan Babu wondered for a moment if he should pay him a quarter of a rupee more, but later dismissed the thought. That really would have been spoiling him. After years he got two new shirts tailored and also bought a pair of new slippers.

Damayanti's mother too, liked his visits. With him she would discuss her late husband's love for music and the days gone by. She said that her Damodar had taken after his father in his passion for music. Why, a few days ago, when someone in his office had said something derogatory about classical music, he had nearly hit the poor man on the face.

"Don't get taken in by his gentle ways, Bhaiji," the mother twinkled at him.

Madhusudan Babu could see that she was proud of her son.

"How could I help it?" Damodar protested, embarrassed. "The man was insisting that Sooha and Sughrai are two separate raags."

Madhusudan Babu supported him wholeheartedly.

"These days, Madhusudanji," Damodar went on, "people go to four concerts, listen to All India Radio mornings and evenings, and claim they are musicologists. No music in their ears, nor rhythm. But who cares? All you need to do is manipulate a few newspaper editors, get a few people to talk about you in loud tones and there you are, a venerable music critic!"

Madhusudan Babu could have embraced him.

Whenever Damayanti's name came up, the old mother began to weep. "Her stars are bad, see, what else can one say? Her father had taken such care to get her a good groom. The family, the lineage, the job, everything was carefully checked and double checked. But when even Raja Janaka couldn't foretell Sita's fortune, who can decipher what the stars have decreed? Exactly six months after her marriage, her husband died in a street accident. The loss of their only child killed his parents soon after, and since then our little girl has become a sanyasin. Earlier she spoke a little, but since she has taken up this new task, she just opens her mouth to say Yes or No. She's as gentle as a cow, Bhaiji, as gentle as a cow."

The old woman would then weep some more and go on to blame her crippled body, which had tied up her children hand and foot to the sickbed. Such a good and respectable job Damayanti had, but she left it behind to come and nurse her mother. Now even when she prayed for death the gods turned a deaf ear to her prayers. Thank God for Madhusudan Babu's visits, she said, often. When he came, the gloom departed for a few hours, otherwise earlier it was just the three of them and the four bleak walls around. The fates had indeed decreed otherwise, or else this house should have been full of people, of activity, of children. No? The old woman would heave a sigh. After a while Damayanti would come and feed her. She would then help her rinse and put a cardamom or a clove in her toothless mouth, gently admonishing her, "You've talked enough. Now close your eyes or the fever will go up."

For all the gentle care, Madhusudan Babu could not see the poor old mother getting any better. Damodar was worried because the doctors did not give her more than a few months. "I'm asking Damayanti to apply for her old job. She has taught at that college for sixteen years, they must take her back. What will she do here after mother is no more? I shall go to Haridwar once this is all over. My guru's ashram can take me in."

Madhusudan Babu felt a leaden weight choking him.

"She, of course, says that the people on the school managing committee back there are old-fashioned conservative people, specially where women teachers are concerned. She feels very suffocated there."

"So?"

"I only hope she won't find it hard to pick up where she left off."

"She could stay here."

"That will be crazy," Damodar burst out, irritably. "There's simply no scope in this town. There she knows the people better and I also need to be relieved of this dead weight of family matters. My guru has been beckoning me for so long. Had it not been for mother, I'd have gone three years ago."

"Won't she feel alone?"

"What is loneliness?" When Damodar smiled a dry smile, his face began to resemble Damayanti's. "Is she any less lonely here?"

"And me, what becomes of me?" Madhusudan Babu wanted to ask, but got up to leave.

A fearful tornado raged within him. So Damayanti will also leave, he said to himself, as he lay upon his sleepless pillow. Damayanti's soft oval face, gentle and sad as an early morning raag, swam before his eyes. In this enormous city there was no place for her, she must leave even if she is reluctant to . . . can't he ask her? . . . Shiva! Shiva! He turned over angrily. Was he in his senses? He must be at least twenty years older than her. But Damayanti's quiet shadow leaned into his thoughts. Her well-oiled braid, her rhythmically-moving rounded buttocks as she walked before him, her beautifully shaped thighs like the trunk of a banana tree. Shiva! Shiva! What was he thinking?

Madhusudan Babu washed his face with cold water and began to polish his tanpura vigorously.

A month later, the old woman died. Madhusudan Babu walked with the bier to the cremation ground. The three of them sat, enveloped in silence, day after day. The brother and sister had folded into themselves. There was nothing left to mourn aloud, was there?

After about a week of this, Damodar gave him the news that he had been dreading. Damayanti had heard from an old friend in her college. There was a vacancy. If she wanted to, she could return.

Madhusudan Babu felt as if his legs were made of lead as he traced his way home.

He lay thinking till late at night.

The next morning he went to the bank and withdrew some money, then he went to the older part of the city where no one knew him, traced out a shop that gave old typewriters on hire, and brought one home. The shopkeeper asked for a hundred and fifty rupees towards a security deposit which he paid. On the way home he bought some plain paper and an envelope.

The old, out-of-practice fingers took some time to even sit comfortably on the keys, but eventually, he managed to type out a letter to the chairman of Damayanti's old college. It was a vile, vulgar letter. It alleged that Damayanti had been behaving like a harlot. It accused her of having an affair with one Madhusudan Babu. It described their intimacies in vulgar detail. The letter ended with a polite request that such a one who slept around with a man old enough to be her father should not be taken back into an honored institution like theirs. It was signed—"A Well Wisher."

Having completed the letter, Madhusudan Babu folded it neatly. He put it in the envelope. He typed out the address. He cleaned his house thoroughly and then hired a rickshaw and left for the railway station.

It had been many years since he had been there. He cast a few furtive glances here and there to make sure that he was not being observed. There was no one about whom he knew. He bought himself a ticket for the next town, keeping his face averted. He sat behind a newspaper till the train came to a halt at the next station. He got off the train, came out of the railway station and, having put the letter in the letter box outside, bought a ticket for the return journey.

Once back, he went to his neighboring temple. He sat there then, listening to the holy chants.

THE HIJRA

Kamala Das

Translated by the author

In Sion-Koliwada, a suburb of Bombay, there is a colony where only hijras live. Among the huts with corrugated iron roofs and the garbage heaps where vegetable peelings lie rotting, you can see hermaphrodites and eunuchs resting on charpoys or squatting under breadfruit trees, smoking beedis. Though dressed in saris, most of them have stubble on their faces.

Whenever a male child is born in the city or around it, the hijras rush to the child's house to do their customary dance of benediction. In return, the women of the house present these dancers with wheatflour, coconuts, rice and jaggery. The hijras hate miserliness. If anyone annoys them, they lift their skirts and exhibit their pitiable genitalia. For the viewers this sight is like the worst of insults. When the hijras pass with their drums and jingling anklets, women turn timid all of a sudden, flinging coins at them and moving away in haste. Their timidity and squeamishness amuse the eunuchs who turn back to stare and laugh. Their jokes are always obscene and ribald. The eunuchs prefer white cotton saris but the hermaphrodites sport nylons and voluminous skirts. There are many people in Bombay who believe that the hijras kidnap children and maim them to convert them into eunuchs. You will never be able to find an eyewitness, though. After all, who would want to incur the displeasure of that dangerous tribe? However, children do get kidnapped. Or else, how does one explain the inexhaustible population of the Koliwada hijra-colony?

This colony's undisputed chief was Ramkinkari, known as Rambhau. A dark six-footer, he was always in a white sari. Whenever he condescended to smile, yellow teeth—like large tombstones—protruded from a betel-stained mouth. In the evenings Rambhau liked to be given an oil massage by his favorite hermaphrodite, the plump Sakubai. For this pleasurable ritual, Rambhau would stretch his lanky frame on a charpoy. Sakubai rubbed Brahmi oil into the sunburned skin and kneaded the meager flesh as though she were preparing dough for rotis. Rambhau only grunted while she talked. After the massage he would get up and pace in the pale moonlight, giving counsel to the residents who asked for it.

It was on such an evening that an old woman from the city came to him. She wore her sari the Gujarati way. She wore no jewelry. Even her earlobes were bare. Her eyes had a brilliance that suggested lunacy.

The old woman stopped near Rambhau's charpoy and stared at him.

"Who is this old woman? Where has she come from?" Sakubai asked, pausing to look at the visitor.

"You cannot come here," said Rambhau, not bothering to rise. "Nobody can enter this colony without my permission."

The old woman smiled. She sat on the ground and stretched her legs in front of her. "I am tired," she said. "I left my home early in the morning."

"Where is your home?" asked Sakubai.

"My house is on Warden Road," the old woman said. "I forgot to carry money with me so I could not travel by bus. I walked all the way. I have sworn not to return home without finding my daughter."

"Your daughter?" asked Rambhau. "What is the use of looking for your daughter in a hijra-colony? Only the likes of us live here."

"She is a hijra," said the old woman. "She was born seventeen years after I got married. I had to go on pilgrimage to several shrines before I could conceive. But when she arrived, she was a hijra. God made her that way. But her face was radiant like the full moon. I named her Poonam. She had a birthmark shaped like a conch on her cheek. My astrologer told me that the birthmark was very auspicious. It would make the family very wealthy, he said . . . but my mother-in-law could not forgive me for delivering such a baby. My husband hated the child. Then your people stole her when she was asleep in her cradle."

"You are wrong," said Rambhau. "We do not steal babies. We buy them, paying handsomely. We have a rigid code of ethics, mother."

"When did you lose that baby?" asked Sakubai.

"This Diwali will be the eighteenth since her birth. It was on the eve of Diwali that she was kidnapped. I was taking a bath in the servants' bathroom . . . "

"Were you a servant then?" asked Sakubai. "I thought you were from a rich Gujarati family."

"I am," said the old woman. "But after Poonam was born they treated me badly. They hid me and my child in the servants' quarters. I was afraid that they would strangle my baby. I would stay awake at night to guard her."

Rambhau rose majestically from the charpoy. He peered into the old woman's face and grunted, "Your child must have died. She is certainly not in this colony."

"I shall not return home till I have found my daughter," said the old woman.

"You have no right to stay here. This is a colony for hijras," said Sakubai.

At that moment, with the tinkling of anklets, the soft thumping of drums and the swish of skirts, a group of hijras arrived, carrying large cloth bundles which they placed before Rambhau. He opened the bundles and scrutinized the contents. He grunted, then said, "This old woman wants to find her daughter who was stolen from home eighteen years ago."

The group listened to him in silence.

"She says that her daughter was as radiant as the moon and had a birthmark on her cheek resembling a conch."

"It must be our Rugma," said a hijra. "Rugma is fair. She has a birthmark on her left cheek."

"Stop talking like a stupid woman," shouted Rambhau.

"There is no such person here," said another hijra.

"You had better go back. It has turned dark already," said Rambhau.

The old lady merely nodded.

"Old woman, we don't want the police to come here looking for you. Go back to your home in Warden Road," said Sakubai.

"Yes, we don't want the police here," said the hijras.

"I shall not return home without my daughter," said the old woman, stretching herself on the ground.

"Don't lie on the ground. It is going to rain this evening," said Rambhau.

"You cannot live here," said Sakubai.

"If my daughter can live here, I can too," said the woman. "I am an excellent cook. I shall make patrel, dhoklas and khandwi for all of you. If you have some ghee I shall fry onions and cook khichri for you."

"You are a rich lady. How can we make you cook khichri for us?" asked Sakubai.

"Nobody in my home loves me. My mother-in-law calls me the mad one. Whenever she sees me she spits and hurries to take another bath," said the old woman.

"Your mother-in-law must be very old. She will die soon. After her death you will be happy. Then nobody will call you mad," said Sakubai.

Rambhau walked towards a well. Drawing water, he began to wash his chest. The sound of the pulleys soothed the old woman's nerves. She closed her eyes.

"Are you hungry?" asked Sakubai.

The old woman did not answer.

"If I were to bring you two rotis and some cooked vegetables, would you eat those?" asked Sakubai.

"What is the use of asking her?" said Rambhau, his voice rising above the cool sound of water. "Give her something. She is obviously hungry."

"Rugma, bring a few rotis here for this old woman," shouted Sakubai.

A pretty young woman opened a window and looked out. "Old woman? Why has she come here?"

"She is a Gujarati lady from Warden Road, looking for her lost daughter," said Sakubai.

Rugma came out of her tenement and gazed at the old woman lying on the ground. The moon lit up the pretty young woman's face making it seem unbelievably beautiful. The studs on her earlobes gleamed.

"Rugma go back to your cooking," shouted Rambhau.

"Let me stay here in the moonlight for a few minutes, Rambhau. I am tired. I have danced for hours on the hot, concrete floors of some Ghatkopar homes," pleaded the young woman. "If you make me dance without rest, I shall die before Diwali."

She was wearing a red cotton skirt. The silver border on its edge resembled the moonlit tides on the Arabian Sea. The old woman stared at the silver border as though mesmerized. Rugma's birthmark was livid in the moonlight. The woman rose and stumbled towards Rugma. "How old are you?" she asked.

"She is twenty-six," shouted Rambhau. "Besides, she is from Mysore. She came here only four years ago. She cannot be your daughter."

"Who is your mother?" asked the old woman, peering into Rugma's face.

"The earth is my mother. Bhoomi Devi. Yes, the earth is my mother," said Rugma.

She turned round and round fluttering her pale hands.

"They are like white doves," said the old woman.

Yes, the girl certainly seemed to resemble Poonam.

Rambhau, scrubbed clean and smelling of Lifebuoy soap, began to beat the dholak in tune to Rugma's dance.

The throb of the drum affected the old woman like the approach of a migraine. The moonlight brightened. The brass of the moon, seen above the huts and the dusty breadfruit trees, suddenly turned into gold. Emeralds seemed to hang suspended from the branches of the trees.

Oh Yellamma, save me from my misery . . . sang Rugma, swaying her hips, her face upturned to receive the light of the moon.

> Oh Yellamma, my body burns.
> Who fashioned a furnace between my thighs?
> Who built a dam across the river of my blood?
> Oh Yellamma, save me from this misery . . .

From the tin-roofed huts, shadows emerged to stand around Rugma. Rugma danced on with her eyes closed. Beads of sweat glistened on her upper lip. The red dust, rising in swirls around her bare calves, began to look gray.

Suddenly, there was the sound of thunder. Then the rain came, meager and smelling of rats' urine.

The old woman's nostrils flared.

"You are not my daughter," she murmured. "My daughter was fair. You are red, red like the earth. You are the daughter of Bhoomi Devi. . . . How did I mistake you for mine?"

When the drums began to rumble again, the old woman mistook the sound for thunder.

She walked as fast as she could, guided only by the blue lights of the Railway Station, while in the distance the sound of Rugma's anklets thinned to silence.

THE WIDOWS OF TITHOOR

Viswapria L. Iyengar

There once were widows in this land who battled ghosts with firewood . . .

They dipped into trunks and pulled out yards of transforming memories. Hummed a snatch of her song while biting rough chunks of pineapple. Cooling betel-clotted mouths, watching nectar smear the earthen floor, they recall, with the menacing twists and turns of a mind which has not seized the importance of a story. It would have been different had there been a temple for Haldi, an image or edict.

They claimed to remember an event that none had witnessed or acknowledged: that the White Ghosts that had then ruled the land had willed her death in the dark pages of night. Fire had been her only grandeur. In that moment close to life and death, Haldi sang of times when a half-light half-dark geometry had been fixed on earth. Woman had broken the law of light to tame fire in her hearth. She had stolen it from the elements.

A furious wind had blown through Tithoor that night. And it sucked her ballad into stone lungs, shedding boughs of jasmine into swamp basins where black buffaloes communed with mosquitoes. Sampige flowers fell into nests, beheading baby sparrows with petals. Hailstones caused newborn goats to die of fever. The elements too had been part of night's nemesis.

For many days they had not understood the significance.

Four sons had been stillborn to Haldi.

Her pockmarked Ramanna had died the year merchants from Saurashtra had set up stall at the big cattle fair. . . . Copper pots engraved like jeweled ornaments, mirror-embroidered skirts and blouses, davinis of peacock colors, sunset-orange peels, thick black iron pans, rolling pins slender as lacquered kolattai.

Widow Haldi had blossomed after the fair.

It was then, a fortnight after Ramanna's sudden death, that she began to live alone on the hill. In a simple mud, wood and thatch hut. It caused a quiver of scandal, her insistence on wilderness.

No husband or sons were there to observe her absence when the fire was not lit and water not boiled the morning after. For the rest, it did not matter. Haldi was a law unto herself.

A bedroll of light divided the night into two equal parts of darkness. The goatherd stretched out on the mothsheet. The Collectorate projected bars of light, out into the Tithoor night.

The Collector had ridden past, hooves shaking off wet clumps of earth on the bedsheet of light. Paler than ever before, with lips that bore the smell of blood, he looked strange, an anamic Asura.

Khaki shirt torn, the Sahib had, as usual, not spoken the dialect . . . he just ordered, in English, with a deathlike coldness. So the goatherd was not sure if this was an apparition or. . . . Perhaps the Asura would ride back into the forest. Then he would be sure to get a good look at his face.

The goatherd collected stories during nights without hairy black ears, and told them back to himself during his long marches. He saw prim English soldiers fall down like mud pots in the valor of his fantasy. He walked on the hairpin bend, a flexible kind of sway accommodating every rock or clump of thorns. He missed his flock. He pretended to be glad to be rid of his goats but it irked him to have no one to talk to. He looked forward to his solitude, and then, in the quiet, he became so loquacious that it hurt. He walked with a slouch. Whipping up his pole, he thrashed pineapple-cactus leaves. . . . "Sule maga Engleesh. I am not afraid of that butter on your face." And knocked off the roughly-cut jack pole, which otherwise guided idiot nibblers over the hills and through the plains.

Lights in the Collectorate were subdued and the empire now rested on pinpoints of illumination. The ceiling of the room where Collector Williams officiated was high enough to have allowed coconut palms to grow to their full height. Here the furling and unfurling of parchment had the crisp bearing of currency notes. During the day, the atmosphere was blank, in an arithmetic of punctuated breathing. As if bad temper would unleash war. Cannons had begun to inhabit the landscape. They stood like watchdogs at the gates. Among themselves the clerks, darwans and peons composed treatises on the nature of this White Ghost. Now, in response to the Sahib's twilight privacy, they had retired to prescribed zones.

The white colonial bungalow sprawled, an enchanted oasis. Williams looked out of the huge windows in the first floor study. Wood smoke spiraled. He pressed the lion-seal in the damp hollow of his palm, paced the floor in measured steps. Sat down on the Turkish carpet by the window, a tree trunk of files. He did not want to be observed looking out at the hills. Picking up of local gossip did not entitle the night-watchman to clamor for his attention.

He arranged the files fanlike, a perfect symbol of connection. The civil service spread out, the army stood in a tall pile. But it did not calm him now to elucidate delicate threads that wound the Raj together. The fan had a more carnal significance, evocative of damsels dedicated to a lusty god, tranquilizing guilt and domination. He should have gone further East, perhaps to China. It was different here.

The watchman was asleep. Collector Williams was glad to be alone to watch the hailstones, to discern the lisping of a human voice in the midnight gale.

Tithoor was a little village in the Deccan Plateau. It ran along the lines of the three-pronged Muthanna Dwarf Hills. A forest of sandalwood and jackfruit cropped out of the Gandhitopi Hills. On the eastern plains were the Collectorate, police station, dispensary farms and dwellings. To the west were huge boulders of magnificent shapes. In this stout barren landscape, the widows built a universe of rituals. Inside a carved rock—half-cave, half-tomb—was a flat white stone, four lines etched on it.

The widows believed that the claws of goddess Huliamma had marked the stone. They offered her braided wild flowers, herbs and any beast or creature they were able to hunt. When winds slaked the hills, they twined garlands of weeds and splattered the white stone with the blood of snakes or toads. They dried fur and skin to stitch purses with colored threads and seed beads. Huliamma was their creation. The widows did not cower or pretend before their deity. She was asked only to sanctify a power that was already theirs.

Sunshine glazed granite. Tirthamma, Nunganna's widow, was to be initiated into the fold. Gigiakka combed her thin wavy hair. After running the long comb down, she would crush the teeth together between thumb and forefinger. Hearing the crispness in the slices of wood, she would grin. Fingers pounced excitedly on an errant louse walking over Tirthamma's round shoulders and killed it with a tick of her thumbnail. On calciated wrinkles blood flecked rust.

Nellamma sat on a warm lap of rock. Her damp sari held flowers and leaves in a moist pouch. She was braiding long loops. Later she would tie them up in a tobacco leaf and set it afloat in the pond. Tirthamma was not beautiful; if she had been, Nellamma would have climbed further to cut a lotus. Not for the hair, too heavy, it was a god's flower. Haldi could decorate the sacrificial beast. Nellamma yawned. She would go to the pond, sleep in the scented shade of the sandal. She gave Gigiakka crushed petals.

Tirthamma was past middle age, had borne six children and was a grandmother as well. Her body bent in the cycle of womanhood, she labored in the fields under the blazing sun. Now she was a widow and would join the group.

Tirthamma was fortunate. Now she would not die nameless in the desert of her labors. Tonight she would let her soul speak.

Before the initiation, the body had to be balmed. Bony hands massaged Tirthamma's scalp, smearing the cool pulp of petals into the roots of her hair. The fetus of a sparrow had been ground with raw papaya. They bound Tirthamma's feet with the paste. It would make worn arches sensitive to grass, evening sand.

The ceremony was after nightfall. Haldi would conduct the rituals.

"Why build on the plains, carrying wood so far away? My home will be the wilderness."

Haldi lived on the hill. She enjoyed solitude. The tigress delivered her cubs in the ravines and Haldi's ballads were born on the hill.

Haldi worked in a brahmin zamindar's house as a bath maid. At dawn she gathered firewood and left for the millhouse. Tucked a bushel of herbs into her sari's fold. Chewed a neem stick down the hill. Between astringent spit and the fruity taste of sleep, she murmured a ballad.

She ground the herbs in a stone mortar behind the cowshed. Filled a huge earthen boiler with thirty brass pots of water from the well. Packed the furnace with logs and cowdung cakes and lit the fire, coaxed it to spread, blowing gusty pipes. Through the metal cylinder, air echoed like wind on the sand.

She massaged children and ladies with thick castor oil. Hands slid, honey-like, over aching limbs, and even the flaccid flesh of cow-milking grandmothers felt aroused. She bathed them one by one. The children, a whole monkey army, she bathed in groups of four. Then she lit coals and sprinkled lumps of sambrani, placed a basket over it, and helped the ladies—tied-up mummies in old soft saris—spread their tresses out over the scented smoke. Opiated, they lay with half-shut eyes and discussed family matters.

Sometimes, when she was bathing children, the zamindar, Anjayya, would open the bathhouse door. She taunted him, "Go, devil-goat, or I won't pour another pot of water on your child."

Brahmins were always afraid of children catching the chill. The old man would wish God had not poured so much sharp sauce into her brain, shut the door and walk away.

This was the substance of the work that fed her. The forest was enough for food, but not for jaggery, oil and cloth. The brahmin ladies did not chat with her as they did with other maids, did not toss her any morsels of gossip. They were afraid, curious. If it had not been for her hands they would not even have allowed her to work. She affected them with a strange ennui that caused panic.

Haldi caricatured the zamindar and his family. Many evenings passed in the heady flavor of her tales. Her ability to spill mirth and thought was the widow's prized possession.

Feet baking in a mound of paste, Tirthamma sat on a palm leaf.

Lips, frozen in disbelief, melted into a pool of vowels. A deer ran, in fawn stitches, through pillars of bark. Oiled fingers moved in the serrations of palm. Polished hooves of light. Like sudden rain, the temple bells of Tithoor rang delicate.

> Wild jasmines, weave the wind with the stars.
> Crown my flowing hair.
> Sun, smudge your evening blood on my forehead.
> Mother Moon, I will swim . . .

The windless morning carried Haldi's initiation ballad to the widows adorning Huliamma's cave. Released from fatigue, they squinted in the sudden light, laughter creasing out notches of strain.

> . . . with your silver scales in the river.
> I will eat crystal sugar and drink date wine. For
> tonight I am bride unto myself.

Tirthamma pleased them. When a novice entered the fold, neither she nor the widows knew how she would grow. The circle would insist that she find the truth about herself, as the seed knew of its oil and the rock of its metals. Eyes fixed on a distended profusion of jackfruit she sang, oblivious of the watching widows.

They saluted their High Priestess. Haldi had said, "Older the woman, more elaborate the ritual. The spirit will have to be lifted out of greater darkness. This is necessary, for the pain of years will make the dance more agile."

If Haldi knew that Nellamma had thought of the lotus but given Tirthamma only crushed petals for oil, she would have censured her and sent her back to the hill. Nellamma liked the wisdom of rituals, it soothed her, but she had not Haldi's physical tenacity. She played with the curly yarn of guilt and dismissed the bloom from her mind.

Tirthamma sang Haldi's earliest ballad:

> Darkness, Goddess of pain,
> knows not of bodies male, female.
> She searches, breast of night,
> for spirit, for soul.
> He sleeps, I awake
> and follow her to the jackfruit grove.
> Gauche feet, they dance to the jackal's howls,
> braiding the rope that beats me.
> Breast of night, Goddess, feel the truth of me.

Afraid of the sudden music, afraid of the perfume that had been burned into her hair, Tirthamma stood up split the cast of paste and ran. Heavy brown ankles carried her gracefully into the heart of the forest.

The widows watched, understanding, for one such afternoon or night they too had come to fear the power in themselves. They walked over the western face of the hill without speaking.

Anjayya, the zamindar, opened and shut the doors of the bathhouse many times, but steam did not cloud his bifocals. The faint effluvia of yesterday's herbs lingered in the drains. Through a missing tile, the sun shone on the brass swell of the cauldron. The cold-stone floor, smoothed fine by oil and water, tormented him; wet breasts of the long-limbed women haunted the room. Today the huge clay boiler had not been lit, the bronze one had sufficed.

The zamindar ate a three-course meal, burped in prescribed gastric measure. The room had been darkened to a fetal quietude. Windows shut. He lay down beside his wife on the reed mat, caressed her belly, soft wasted looseness. And encysted declining masculinity in the dough of motherhood. She did not smell of Haldi. He asked why her hair did not smell of sambrani.

"She did not come for work. Who does she wait upon in that hill hut, I wonder. . . ? One night, she told me, a deer ran in and licked her feet. . . . She thought its wet nose was a snake. . . . Some rebel from Pithoor visits her. They say he is good-looking, but crude. Still, she could have told me she was not coming. The whole house had to bathe in spoons of water, like crows."

Anjayya thought his wife strange. She wore Dharmavaram silk saris with heavy gold borders, but used worn-out string for her blouse.

"The children were not bathed today. What is a bath without oil and herbs? Washing in hot water and still feeling cold."

He flecked out a grain of betel-nut stuck in his molars.

"Whole morning I was breaking my back making twenty jars of lemon-pepper pickle. A good bath would have stood me well."

Anjayya felt that the least he could do after all these years was listen to his wife. Moreover, it excited him when she spoke of Haldi. They made love in the stupor of late afternoon.

Through the sleepy afternoon work ensued as usual. Williams scratched whorls of India ink with his eagle quill. Arranged the complexity of the events in neat planes of argument. There was dexterity involved in ruling a race that laid great claims to culture. Where barbarism was camouflaged in the nuances of diverse customs. In the sluggish warmth of midday, guilt eased to dull remorse. The fire on the hill was long since cold and unburned logs lay around.

He had sometimes, with disregard for convention, walked his Alsatians at night to the M.D. Hills. Seen her silhouette amongst trees. Last time, she had spoken to him because of the dogs. Native beauty did not soften him. Words froze the moment she spoke. A xylophone of icicles.

The watchman had filed an exhaustive report on the nature and form of her relationship with Veerappa, the rebel leader from Pithoor. He always came at night on a brown horse and stayed till dawn. Her lamp burned oil through the night. Through thin walls, their words were audible as birds in a tree. They spoke about the widows, the zamindar and his family, the peons and clerks in the Collectorate. Long sentences about solitude and aloneness, poetry and justice. He saw shadows, giants, at a respectful distance. At dawn the rebel leader would touch Haldi's feet before mounting his horse. Veerappa came every other full moon.

The watchman was emphatic. There was no sexual suggestion in their relationship. They forgot sexuality in the urgency of communication.

That could only mean that Haldi was a political accomplice, thought Williams. He was perplexed by the reports of abstinence. Forced to deal with the organization of widows, he did not like unannotated cults.

The watchman had rambled on. Haldi had said the Collector was a corncob, his hair the color of corn fiber. The rebel had laughed heartily. One of the widows' husbands had been a night watchman. The widow had related the exercise of information gathering at her initiation. A lot of nonsense about ghosts buying up the eyes of their own people. Becoming blind to the heart, spies of children's weaknesses.

When she looked admiringly at his dogs, and then at him, as if he were a bleached carrot, he felt cold and humiliated. Without fuss he asked about the organization of widows, and whether she intended to continue the diabolical ritual of celebrating the deaths of husbands.

Haldi scorned his ability to delve into her involvements. In trancelike rhetoric she had said, "I am a widow and that is my power."

When he implored her that she owed him an explanation, she did not answer, her silence receding into the dark contours of the three-pronged hills.

Williams told her firmly to disband the organization and sever her connection with Pithoor. Then she would be unharmed.

Haldi laughed, "Collector, Sir, to your mind which has paled under English skies, are not our mangoes bizarre?"

What did mangoes have to do with rebels? He walked back, crossing the sleeping goatherd. The dogs sniffed at clumps of moss and crunched out snails. A fatal sense of futility overtook him and he turned pages in his mind, structuring his dispassion.

He returned to the Collectorate where news of minor but embarrassing insurgencies around the district awaited him. The courier's pale face, littered with the upsurge of adolescence, his steady blue eyes, stirred up forgotten warmth. He offered the boy tea and listened to his enthusiastic description of the ride. His boyish candor made Williams feel urgently protective of his entire race.

As hooves clattered off into the distance he nestled in the womb of his morocco leather armchair and studied the despatches with grave concern. The fire crackled through the night warming the furry toes of his bedroom slippers. The nights were cold and windy.

The days were warm. The air was still. The punkah man was eating paan. Must tell the chap not to spit in the fish pond. Though the man read no English, Williams felt unnerved in his flapping presence, a part of some absurd play with that chap directing from backstage. . . . *The diabolical rituals of the Widows of Tithoor are not unlike those of our witches of yore. . . . In addition, they threaten the religious customs of the landed population. In reverence to the Hindu tradition it is the custom here, before every marriage, to hold a puja in honor of a woman who had died before her husband, to venerate her spirit. All the woman's favorite dishes are cooked and an elderly unwidowed lady is honored with a silk sari and other gifts.*

Collector Williams deleted the above deviation, it was irrelevant. . . . *I have not the least doubt that any action, official or unofficial, will cause not even token resentment in the local population.*

Pomegranate juice from Kabul mixed with the charcoal spittle of a Tithoor peasant. The sun sometimes set that way.

In a muted slurp of gravy, the widows finished the evening meal. They moved in a rivulet of practiced motions, dancers awaiting exit. Colors fell in small squares through earthen windows.

With impatient drops of water, they hushed hearths and walked towards Huliamma at nightfall. Expecting the unknown, a puppet theater from a faraway town, with different gods and demons.

The widows sat down in a circle. Softening mouths in slurring, sleep-waking thoughts.

"Not prayers, but your own expressions in your own voice, to find your own taala. To seek the language of your own peace."

When the widows looked at her, puzzled yet believing, Haldi was cryptic. "Clay glistens like distant lands at the potter's feet. The potter waits for clay to dance."

There had been times when stone words had come out from ancient volcanoes. Her face lit in the brilliance of a hundred temple lamps. A smile of incense and rose petals.

Huliamma's cave of dried gold welled out like an empty eyelid. Stalagmites of time, devoid of tears. The pulse of myths, dreams, perceptions mixed, stretching towards the horizon, dome of the future.

Tirthamma and the acolyte sat on rock seats. Voices receded into the iron silence of night. In a play of music the two women communicated to each other, at first gently, like tiger cubs. With words, sounds and mudras, probing the dampness of a reservoir. Tender detectives of hope.

In a kinship wrought of ritual, they enacted the cycle of womanhood. The birth of a girl-child whom none wanted. On a small drum of stretched deer-skin, Gigiakka beat a rhythm of sleepwalking fingers. The old woman had kept youth and age, fear and peace balanced between her two fingers. Tirthamma enacted childhood.

Adolescence, childbirth, motherhood, old age. The circle mourned each momentary violence. Of wonder beheaded, limbs of youth amputated . . . it moaned every death. Despair forged images of every form. Red berries on a child's face, smallpox. Dilated delivery numbed in the indifference of the arrack walls.

To repeat the widows' words was an autopsy of anguish.

As the two women paused, the circle chanted, "The curse will break and Tirthamma will awake in our fold."

Primordial actors held the stage, enacting the immaculate. Words pounded spices of a unique predicament. They spoke of loneliness, of hallucinations which made adult perception a medium of madness. Of ethereal hope, placentas floating in swamps sprouting lotus blooms.

Tirthamma wandered back to the genesis of her script. From the bowels of the earth she stood up to say, "I am not rock, I am a wound."

Boulders soaked the moonlight through pores of mica, they seemed to stand witness to time itself. Tirthamma's eyes splintered through the moist bark of Gigiakka's face, past hills, night green tresses, "Not wounds, humans . . . "

Haldi had not yet come. The widows missed her in a distracted way, thinking of roasted meat on a windy night. Perhaps she chased a beast across the forest.

Tirthamma stood, purple-black sari clasping stoutness, dark-ebony arms clucking wood and brass bangles, "I was fire, earth and water. I was labor, fruit. . . . The eclipse is past . . . "

If the morning had been deep, night surpassed it with glory. Faces relaxed. The circle unfurled. Women laughed in the midst of battles, ate crystal sugar and drank date wine.

Gigiakka drunkenly embraced Tirthamma and teased her about the lice in her hair. The new widow retorted, "Of all parasites they bother me the least."

Gigiakka fell, dribbling wet warm laughter down the crisscrosses of her face, "You have bubbles of fermented curd on your tongue."

Worried, hardworking peasants brewed a quietness. The sands are cool, pungent with the waft of sandal, herbs and rich soil. The mission of the evening was laid aside and they had earned the leisure of being themselves.

Haldi was a hunter. It was her honor to hunt beast or owl. The days she menstruated she caught fish in the river, astute and agile with her net as with her spear. For an initiation they should eat something "fat and full of blood," she insisted. But it had never taken Haldi this long. Perhaps tonight she would surpass herself.

They watched the mouth of the forest. In liquid moonlight firm-muscled thighs would prowl the forest choosing, pursuing a victim.

Her entry was always a moment of quiet triumph. Sari folded up like a toddy-tapper. Elbows splattered with blood and damp-dark earth. Face that had molded its planes in weighing life. Spotted deer over her shoulders like a quilt. Dead countenance against frayed vitality. There seemed to be a pact. Death sealed the pact. Life reflected upon itself. The thumb of her right hand coiled around a peacock neck, twilight-wings, trailing-thighs, sweeping-sand. Some inverse relationship to Saraswati from whose veena they preened auspiciousness.

The widows prepared the sacrificial fire to cook meat with herbs. They were impatient. Huliamma's hunger had to be appeased. But that Huliamma's will was their own was no secret.

Gigiakka and Tirthamma unhooked spears and walked towards the forest. "Not toads or snakes," the widows shouted loudly. Gigiakka spat curses with her toothless mouth.

The goatherd loitered in the lawns, the watchman kept a sleep-amused eye on him. Through patterned glass he could see the Collector's silhouette feather-writing on a cot-like desk. He missed having someone to talk to, the bleat of listeners.

He had seen a woman burned on the hill and knew the Collector had turned Asura. He had checked the bones. But the goatherd did not know if this too was not part of his delusions.

Did they think of words and orders when they pulled feathers out of dead eagles? The Collector continued quilling.

The goatherd liked the titter near the fish pond. He fell asleep watching wisps of silver glide, disappearing with a twitch of fins. His beedi still, half-smoked.

The last occurrence of the widows celebration rite was after the stated death of Muni-aswamy a night-watchman in the District Collectorate. On many occasions Muniaswamy had proved a reliable and valuable source of information. While his discretion did not match his aptitude to assess local sentiment, he was loyal and of sound health. The deceased, however, had communicated matters of importance to his spouse, who is now a member of the Widows' Organization. It is established that the Widows of Tithoor are in regular contact with the rebels of neighboring districts, Nyoor and Pithoor. . . . It is my

personal opinion that the organization conceals concerted efforts by insurgents to under-
mine the effectivity of the District Administration . . .

Williams pressed the seal. Red lacquer crown.

Mucous threads clung on the block. Felt it congeal into an impression. The cream packet pulsated in his palms, a newborn fox cub.

The Governor would commend his farsightedness.

Gigiakka thrust her spear into the moist earth and braced herself step by step, guiding Tirthamma through the path of animals. Following sounds, twigs snapping, feathers rustling, tongues lapping water in nooks and pools. It was dark except for oil patches of moonlight, the sleeping stillness of white lizards. Shadows spun a sanctuary.

Tirthamma wanted to admit the profound attraction she felt for the Tooth-less One. Her emotions flowed in a tense anxiety and she could not compre-hend terrain nor season. She followed quietly with an intense watchfulness. They sat under a tree, the Old One caught her breath.

"There are things which make me fear for Haldi."

Flame-patterned wings fluttered in the distant rim of vision.

Tirthamma asked, "But why, Old One? They say she is the Goddess of strength."

Gigiakka curved her neck back, swallowing phlegm, "She is condemned not to speak. Of her own powerlessness. The water carrier cannot tell you that the pool is dry. Haldi is afraid. She is being hunted."

"Haldi never misses an initiation, for her a novice's words are Huliamma's breath. The widows sometimes do not heed Haldi because they forget the meaning of things. I feel that she is not in the forest, yet the fear is here . . . "

The old woman moved restlessly over a mat of moss-twigs, "Better fowl than toad."

They trailed the wildfowl interior.

"The Collector and that zamindar chase her, they want to seduce and insult her. . . . She does not understand they play different games, she does not even know the scheme of her own plot."

"Haldi is the warrior goddess woken from the sleep of many hundred years, after a battle." The Toothless One bent down to water caught in ropes of tough roots. She drank from her palms, greedily. Wiped lips with thread tassels. "Before gunpowder, before cannon, before there were ships on coins."

The wild fowl led the hunters to its habitat. Before a mate of duller coun-tenance it preened its feathers and spotted comb. Gigiakka hurled the spear. Tirthamma picked up the dead bird and stroked its beautiful wings. She plucked out feathers and dropped them, softly, along the moonlit path crossed by shadows of branches. They floated in a mute whisper of brown and yellow.

Tirthamma asked simply, "How do you know, Old One?"

Gigiakka was as distant as the stars. She appeared to have crossed the battle-line of memory.

Armies of swords, horses trampled the forest with torches swaying in the wind, lighting trees to dust. Suddenly life was a river of fire. The earth was shaved clean as a woman's belly. Silence rusted in the hills. Women had gone to battle first, children left at water holes. Fire licked pools dry. Leaving the continuity of the tribe in piles of bone-ash to fertilize the first crop of golden grain.

The Old One twisted root-lips without sound.

They drove the men to the interior, fear scaring them mad. Plundered women to swell wombs with the sperm of the master race. . . . Sometimes in her dreams she saw eye-coins of little ones by the charred pit.

The voices within her would not stop and she could not speak. She resented the privilege of memory without Haldi's poetry.

Feathers fell on an ancient graveyard. The old woman walked slowly, clasping the spear, palm sweating. "They do not recognize power, they assault beauty. . . . They do not know that she has come back to avenge us. Now the White Ghosts from across the seas . . . "

She sat on a rock. Tirthamma plucked a palmful of medicinal leaves, crushed them in her hands.

"The sands too were forest . . . the spears were always kept in the cave."

Tirthamma scraped off the paste on a rock, "But what is it that you fear for Haldi?"

"The zamindar has told her she must stop any gathering of widows in the vicinity of Tithoor. If she does not he will advise the priest to declare her evil and have her driven out of the village. Perhaps they wish to seduce her when she is powerless."

Tirthamma spread the paste on Gigiakka's feet, its green coldness closing painful cracks.

Tirthamma asked quietly, "What do the widows say?"

Gigiakka bent forward, "They do not know."

Tirthamma understood the finality of a full stop, a moment of total darkness.

"Then what is the meaning of our rituals?" With bitterness that the mold of age could scarcely conceal she spoke again, distant as the stars, "Haldi alone knows but does not remember."

Tirthamma had plucked the fowl clean. It lay on her arm, bald as a new child. They saw the fires blazing a welcome at the cave. Intoxicated laughter hit the hunters in waves.

The fowl was laid on the spit. Haldi had still not come. In intoxication the widows did not perceive her absence, in fatigue the hunters did not. Flames leapt into naked flesh in a thousand tongues. The widows warmed their feet on coal-heat.

In the balming of Tirthamma's senses an uncanny clarity had been alerted. She understood the old woman's waylaid sentences. The bliss of morning, the discovery of music and voice, were not her privilege. Toiling on land tore her, breaking stones in the quarry stabbed her mute. But, the fragrance of her hair could only be the perpetual tears of dreams. It could not be.

The absence of Haldi, the magical depth of initiation, charted the night sky, fear turning vision.

She went to the old woman sucking crystal sugar with spit-soaked gums. "I too fear for Haldi. Why has she not come?"

The two women left without tasting the food. Some confused path of mutually agreed suspicion. They left with a will, that there was someone to ask and someone to confront.

But they did not reach the thicket of conclusion. They saw the remnant of a fire, a pyre. The old woman had tripped over a broken white shoulder bone. Blind with ash, she screamed, "They are here again . . . run further into the forest."

Later it was said that Haldi's spirit had intervened and persuaded them to return to the festivities. But the truth was, no one had been asked and no one had been confronted. The widows of Tithoor never ventured to inquire into her disappearance. In their silence, and her songs, some of the story remained.

Collector Williams knew the widows had congregated on the western side, perhaps they suspected or already knew. Now they were only a herd of cows, manageable and pliant.

Celebration of a husband's death was murder, barbaric.

Terror was sealed in the scales of Anglo-Saxon argument. Somnambulant vigilance permitted only a hazy observation of an oriental culture. The report was confidential. It was cautious, checkered. . . . The Governor would flatter his own intelligence, deducing the implications of his speedy action on a matter of subtle importance.

He fingered the red talisman, handed the furry envelope to the courier who rode out of Tithoor at dawn on a black Arab mare.

The jackfruit trees shed their heavy rocklike fruit on the jagged peaks, sweet-pungent fragrance enveloped the hill for many days.

THE SERMONS OF
HAJI GUL BABA BEKTASHI

Qurratulain Hyder
Translated by the author

A ll night long they had been singing qawwalis in Azerbaijani Turkish. Before daybreak, the voices receded in the gray Caucasian mist. I came out of the serai and looked at the sky for the Roc. But instead of that fabulous bird which was to take me home, there came a dove, flying straight from the direction of Mount Ararat. It carried a letter in its beak. It perched itself on top of a samovar which the innkeeper had brought out to the vine-covered courtyard. Then it looked around with its beady eyes till its glance fell on me.

The dove dropped an envelope near me and flew away.

"Hanum, perchance this is a message for you from the Roc. It may have postponed its flight," said the old innkeeper.

"Perchance it is a message from one of the distressed. They are seeking the whereabouts of their loved ones, reported missing. For some reason, I keep getting these epistles all the time," I replied.

"Maybe! There are a lot of wars on, all the time," exclaimed the old man of the Qafqaz, who looked like Tolstoy's Haji Murad. He was contentedly puffing at his hookah. "Which one is this?"

I picked up the letter and read it. I decided that the time had come when, in order to begin the search, I had to go back to the beginning.

Therefore, I took off my everyday mask, bid adieu to the old man and began walking towards the Ararat which stood there glistening, as if it were right in front, while, in fact, it was far away.

I walked all day and crossed many a valley and mountain stream and came upon a twilight spring. It was perhaps the spring of the waters of life where Alexander had met Khwaja Khizr who, like St. Christopher, guides those who lose their way. He also meets his seekers by river banks. As it came to pass, near the spring I did see a blue-eyed faqir saying his prayers. As is the custom of those lands, he wore full boots like the Don Cossacks. His white felt cap and striped smock indicated that he belonged to the vanished fraternity of Bektashi dervishes.

As the sun went down, he finished his prayers and looked up. He saw me and said, "Ya Hoo"—O Eternal One—which was the greeting of the Order. Then all of a sudden he began speaking as though someone had turned on an invisible tape recorder. The dervish said, "I travel by the strange light which is neither of the earth nor of the skies and is made up of the celestial colors of Allah's ninety-nine mystical names. And know that the living are already dead and the dead continue to live and the skulls are singing in luminous caves. When their singing turns into the sound of the seas I return to my cell in the pinewoods and wait. Day and night I turn the grindstone of the fear of the gods and take out the corn from the grindstone of his will. Hanum, what is it that you seek?"

"Effendum," I said respectfully, "I come to you as the emissary of an unknown woman. From her distant river-country she has sent me this message. The waves of my river return again and again but time does not come back. Autumn winds sing in the auburn leaves. Dry twigs crackle and burn and wild ducks are crying in the marshes. Minds continue to live while the bodies have died . . . "

"Two years ago I lost my man and nobody can tell me if he is still in the world of the living or was made to cross over. Madame, you who are roaming the lands of the Turks, you may perhaps come across a man of God who knows . . . "

While I read out the epistle, the dervish folded his hands over his stomach and hung down his head as though in prayer. Then he raised his clear-blue eyes and spoke.

"Hanum, not very far from here, in the land of Hungary, there is—or was —the tomb of my revered ancestor, Haji Gul Baba. Time was when prince and commoner from Istanbul and Bokhara, Tirana and Sofia, trekked on foot to the Carpathians to pray at his shrine. Now Mademoiselle, I go there and come back and tell you what I can tell."

He stood under a cypress tree, his hands tucked inside his overlong sleeves. After a few moments he opened his eyes and said, "I saw things at the holy tomb by the Danube. I saw the past and I saw the future. When my great-grandfather Haji Adnan Effendi accompanied a caravan of diplomats to Cathy, on the way to Yarkand he came across a dervish of the order founded by Bektash Quli—servant of God. The dervish walked a little above the ground, for he was one of those sufis who could fly. And he turned to my great-grandfather and said, Take care. Take very good care. Then he walked into a wayside hospice and simultaneously emerged from the other side and entered the Samarkand Museum. He stands in a glass case of that museum in Samarkand, Uzbek, USSR. His eyes have turned to glass."

I did not fully understand what he meant and, not knowing what else to say, asked this Bektashi sufi his name.

"Haji Selim at your service, Hanum," he said, bowing low. "Come with me. I'll do what I can do for the unfortunate woman."

He picked up his staff and tied a seven-cornered stone in his belt of white wool and began to walk like my shadow, a little ahead of me.

We reached an orchard where a red-roofed hut stood on the green bank of Lake Van. The qalander—which means a soul of pure gold—left me standing on the steps and swept in.

He did not come out for a while. I was scared. I tiptoed to a window and peeped in.

I saw a bare room with a wooden floor and a low ceiling with black rafters. An old French stove made of porcelain stood in a corner. Beside it, there lay a tambura and a flute—which I know represented the spiritual flute of Jelaluddin Rumi. Two identical-looking sufis sat on an Azerbaijani rug. They faced each other and sat in absolute silence.

Then one of them got up and turned towards what was perhaps the direction of Medina in the south, and untied a stone from his stomach and opened a belt made of white wool. And I know that the stone represented the stone tied by the Prophet to his stomach because, being very poor, he often went hungry. And the dervish began to perform a Bektashi rite. He repeatedly made a knot in the belt and opened it, and recited, "I tie up evil and release goodness. And I tie up hunger and un-knot contentment. And I cut my harvest with the sickle of humility and grow old in knowledge and sow the seeds of learning. And I bake my bread in the oven of patience . . . "

I stepped back from the window and raised my face to the sky and shouted another Bektashi prayer, "O Bektash," I cried, "you who have no family tree, who neither begets nor is begotten! O Bektash! You move with the revolving times and can hear the sound of the ant crawling on black stone in dark nights . . . " Then I slowly added my own message, "Only, O Bektash, you do not hear the cries of the oppressed and the exploited . . . "

But my voice was drowned in the chants of Selim Effendi and his spiritual alter ego. They intoned, "O Al-Mustafa. O Chosen One . . . Who always walked under the shade of a luminous cloud. O Prophet . . . have mercy on the world . . . "

The room echoed with the cries of "Karim Allah . . . Ya Hoo . . . "

The next moment, Selim Effendi came out carrying a jar and an earthen cup. And then I also said something quite irrelevant, "Effendum. In my faraway land, in our crumbling old ancestral house, we have a large basement. In the basement there are stacks of old books and an old and cracked French stove made of rose-patterned porcelain. And intellectually inclined mice nibble at the books printed in Constantinople, 1872, London EC4, 1873, and Russell Square, 1952. And once, on a frosty afternoon in his publishers' office in Russell Square, the great sufis of the Feringhees had discussed with me the dancing dervishes. . . . Considering that you are one of them, can you tell me more about your vanished Order. . . ?"

The qalander bowed his head and wept. Then he wiped his tears and said something equally off the point. He said, "Hanum, I cry because in accordance with the law of God, my alter ego will die exactly forty days before my death. What will I do during those forty days? Because he keeps warning me."

Suddenly he shouted, "Ali had said: Whatever is written shall remain."

"Effendum, whatever has been written can be dangerous. Here as well as there, because, every letter, as you know, has its mystical power."

The dervish nodded.

"Look, when that Imam of the time signed his orders, the powerful genie of his name went forth and destroyed. . . . Brains were blown out and bodies torn to pieces. Effendum. . . . Could you please tell me where he is . . . if he is still in the world of the living? What shall I write to her?"

"I told you. Take great care."

"The unknown woman writes, His name was Abul Mansur and he was a painter."

"Didn't he run towards the woods to save his skull?"

"No. The woman writes that he was painting wild ducks by a lotus pond."

"He was being very stupid," Haji Selim replied briefly.

"And thousands ran towards the marshes and forests and riverways. And the earth slipped from under their feet and swords hung over their heads . . . "

"There is no sword except Ali's holy sword, Zulfiqar," Haji Selim replied. I fell silent.

"Was this man alone when the end came?"

"No. It was a festival of death."

"Where did this happen?"

"Everywhere. It happens everywhere all the time, East, West, North, South. For Bektashi has his face in all directions."

Haji Selim Effendi looked at me intently. "Hanum, are you not one of those who believe?"

I made no answer and resumed. "And millions crossed the frontiers. They came in silence from the East and after a while returned in the same silence. Nothing has made much difference to them and they continue to live in misery as always . . . "

"And when nothing much happened even afterwards, I thought—It is written that you get the answers and the inner light if you make the Haj pilgrimage of your own soul. I did so. But found no sort of light."

"You probably have the seal of ignorance on your heart. Now, for the unknown woman's sake I shall do what I can do." He poured a little water from the jar into the cup and recited a Bektashi prayer. "There is no God but God, and Mohammed is his prophet and Ali is his friend and Mehdi is the last Imam and Moses is the word of God and Jesus the spirit of God. . . . Now Hanum, look in the water . . . "

"Why? Have you found the wonderworking Cup of Jamshid?" I asked.

"Hanum, look in the water."

I looked hard and said, "But, Effendum, this has nothing to do with what I am looking for. I only see a horse-drawn carriage. It is crossing a papery, Japanese sort of bridge. And a puppet sits inside, wearing a No mask. And the coachman has no face. Effendum, it seems to be a place near Nara or Kyoto . . . of the Shoguns' times. . . . You know what I mean. . . . Oh well, and it is so quiet you can hear the dew falling on cherry blossoms. Yes, and now a fragile canoe is sailing in the distance on a misty river and there are delicate mountains and a red hut half-hidden in the bamboos and a little man sits in the veranda painting . . . in infinite loneliness. . . . Effendum, I am afraid all this looks suspiciously like Zen . . . "

"Zen is correct too . . . " he said, raising his head. "Look again carefully. Is it a fragile canoe or a tank. . . ?"

"Effendum . . . the water in this cup of yours has turned red."

Haji Selim picked up the vessel and went down to the shore. He threw the cup in the waters of Lake Van and came back wiping his hands on his overlong sleeves. Then he sat down on the steps of the hut and chanted. "I grind the grindstone of the fear of God and tie up evil and release goodness and tie up hatred—Was that person, Abul Mansur, a human being or a symbol?"

"Both," I replied.

Haji Selim bowed his head and began to cry again.

"Shall I write to that woman to bake her bread in the oven of patience?" I asked witheringly. "Effendum, now I return to Shahjehanabad. You may also trek back to Istanbul to your Takia Mevlevi in Pera or Topekapu or the Khanqah Oghlu Ali Pasha."

"Hanum, I have nowhere to go. All the two hundred and fifty-six Takias of Constantinople were closed down by the orders of the Imam of Modern Times. Some of the Takias have their models in the glass cases of the museums of Istanbul," he said, and continued weeping.

"Well, Effendum, wherever you return, tell him that his servants have suffered as in hell. And they continue to suffer. Now you can say your Isha prayers.

"We Bektashis do not simply pray. We crucify ourselves. We call our prayers the crucifixion of Mansur. Day after day I ascend the cross and get down and die and resurrect myself. That is something you will never do. So you will not know. Day after day I tie up impatience and release patience. God is patient because he is eternal. We become impatient because we have short lives."

I said rather irreverently, "Effendum, do you remember Haji Yusuf Bektashi of Spain of many centuries ago? Well, he and his disciples remained patient but that did not help when disaster struck his country and his people . . . "

Haji Selim did not seem to take any notice of my remark and continued, "And I travel by the light of God's ninety-nine beautiful names—Hoo, which is the color of red, and Wahid, which is the color of green, and Aziz, whose light is black, and Wadood, which is non-light. Haji Selim Bektashi's conversation is over."

The invisible tape recorder began to produce weird noises as though it was being played backwards. For, existence is divided into many planes.

Haji Selim had disappeared behind the closed door of his Takia. I tiptoed to the window and saw that the two identical-looking sufis—Selim Effendi and his spiritual alter ego—who had sat facing each other, turned into paper. A gust of wind coming from the Ararat shook the wooden hut and the dervishes blew away and floated around like bits of old yellow paper. The colors vanished into non-light.

The Roc descended on Tughlaqabad and spread its wings. I got off and came into town. I thought, Before I begin the search anew for the unknown woman's man, I must repair my worn-out mask.

The city looked changed although I had not been away long. And I could not find my way to the newest capital on the site of Indraprastha. So I asked a passerby, "O Brother Passerby, can you direct me to a place where I can get my mask repaired?"

"Honorable sister, over the site of Princess Qutluq Nigar Khanum's grave there is an air-conditioned beauty parlor. It is run by one who once appeared in Rider Haggard's novels. She should be able to help you."

So I walked down to this ultramodern building which stood over the grave of Qutluq Nigar Khanum and I saw a big crowd collected in front, as though someone had died. I went inside and saw a lot of bejeweled women sitting in a row, their heads stuck under monstrous machines. More were arriving—the way corpses arrive at the morticians' in the lands of the Feringhees.

I was terrified and rushed back to the street and decided to make do with my old mask. I was accosted by a thin young man with a goatee. He spoke in a flat voice. "O Honorable, confused-looking sister. I am a visitor from a neighboring country. I want to eat. Can you direct me to a place where I can get good river-fish?"

So I took him to an inn buzzing with the phoney foreign accents of men and women who looked alike. As a matter of fact, the women looked like men and the men like coy young girls. It was, I remembered, called the unisex look. Some of the women looked like high priestesses of weird cults.

The foreigner with the goatee sat down at a table and said that although he was a friend and an ally and a guest of the government, he would like to pay for his food. I said, "O Brother ally, I appreciate your sense of self-respect. I notice that you are not overburdened with the sense of self-respect. I notice that you are not overburdened with the sense of gratitude and hold your head high. Tell me, what are you doing in Shahjehanabad, away from your golden land?—A fish out of water as it were."

He looked out of the plate glass window of the inn. Through this window, the crumbling tombs of some of the old Turkish kings of India looked like Royal Academy paintings by Thomas Daniel. Inside some of the tombs, the poor had made their dwellings and were busy cooking their food and living out their sordid lives. Because all is Zen anyway and Bektashi has his face everywhere.

All of a sudden the young man with the goatee began speaking in the voice of Haji Selim Effendi. He said, "The country we have left behind for a while lives in us. The puppets descend on the stage tied to strings. The puppeteer pulls up one and lets down another."

And like Selim Effendi, I answered, "That is also correct."

Then I took out the unknown woman's letters from my bag and said, "Brother, the dead are dreaming of the living and the living of the dead. And the pictures of pictures continue to exist. Since you have come from the river-country, perchance you have heard of the name of the artist Abul Mansur . . ."

The young man continued to eat because food is the greatest single reality between birth and death, beginning and end—although we had been told to tie up hunger and release contentment so that some people could eat more than the others. So I asked the young man, "Why have you come to this patient land of ours and what are you looking for?"

"Is search necessary?" he asked stoically. "I have come here on a scholarship offered to me by your government to learn acting, at which you people are great experts."

"Are you from a family of those who wear masks and pretend to be somebody else? In other words, is your father also an actor?"

"My father painted wild ducks."

"Is he still among the living?"

The young man looked bored. He said, "I suspect that my lady-mother has written to you as well. For the last two years she has been collecting addresses and writing to all sorts of people seeking the whereabouts of my father. She would not believe that my father was taken out of the house at five o'clock in the morning and shot dead. Inquisitive lady, now I take your leave. You can continue to look at your ancient many-layered capital through the windows of this inn."

He rose, and went out, and was lost in the evening crowds of Shahjehanabad.

It had started raining. I came to the window and heard the clutter of hooves. And I saw the horse carriage appear from behind the tomb of Qutluq Nigar Khanum. The carriage passed by and the coachman turned around and looked at me. He, of course, had no face. So I quickly touched my own face and was satisfied that the mask was in place. But I had this odd feeling that I was not even pretending. I was a puppet or a character in a Noh play which nobody understood.

Beloved friends. This is a riddle set before his disciples by Haji Gul Baba Bektashi. He taught through parables ancient and modern, when he lived in his famous hospice by the Danube, six centuries ago.

"And at this stage my melody is over. O Worlds, take your leave and go back . . . " said Maulana Jelaluddin and put down his flute.

I

Jeelani Bano

Translated by Jai Ratan

"It was long past midnight when someone brought the news that Amir was dead. I leapt off my bed like a dark raging cloud and ran out as if I were mad. I prodded and pinched the child's body. Was it really Amir?"

My mother must have told me this story a thousand times and every time I would ask her in an agitated voice, "Amma, Amma, what made you suspect that I was not Amir?"

I had been lost and found. But a fear still lurked in Amma's mind that a child once lost could never be found again. "It could have been some stray child passed on to me just to console me," she would say. Amma's remarks would shake me to the very core.

Could it really be true? Had someone really tricked my mother by palming off some other child on her? Maybe the real "I" was still wandering somewhere in the countryside or some unknown mother was holding "me" in her lap. But then who was "I"? Had I really been lifted from somewhere and carried through the dark of the night to be placed in my mother's lap? Such questions assailed me from all sides till I wanted to scream. So much so that I even started doubting my own existence. I knew of no way to unravel this tangled skein.

When I grew up a little I decided to go in search of this Amir whom, in a fit of forgetfulness, my mother must have left behind sleeping on a train. Once I had even gone to see the railway lines. Oh, Allah, how long the track was! It stretched on and on and did not seem to end anywhere. I did not know where the last station on this line lay—that is, if any such station existed.

Whenever I asked Abba about it, he just laughed. "Silly boy, a railway line never comes to an end," he would tell me. "It's a network that covers the entire country."

Had they laid this network just to keep a child apart from his mother, I often wondered. How long would the poor Amir keep riding the trains? It was indeed so naive of Amma to have accepted me as her Amir without questioning. And then all over again I would agonize over the fact that Amma had some doubts about my identity.

For that matter, even others looked suspiciously at me when I sat in their midst, feeling lost. They would call me by my name but I wouldn't reply, as if this name did not belong to me. Actually, I did not care. Why should I take any notice of them? They were, all the same, amused by my antics. My elder sister would shake her head and ask, "Where were you just now?"

"On the train of course," I would reply and they would start laughing.

Once Amma fell ill. She was in the kitchen making chapatis. Suddenly, she came out of the kitchen and was walking across the courtyard when she fell down in a heap. My elder sister shrieked, and in a moment the courtyard filled with women of the neighborhood. My sister mixed some kind of leavened dough and made Amma drink it. Sabira said that it was so potent that it even brought the dead back to life. But all Amma did was open her weary eyes and give me a cursory look. Then she turned on her side and slid back into sleep.

Many days passed. Every night when I went in to see Amma, I had a strong urge to lie down by her side, but I was put off by her groans. Then, instead of going to her I would dump myself on the pile of dirty clothes and fall asleep. I really felt sore at Amma for not taking any notice of me.

One night when I happened to go to her, she gave me an angry look and said, "Look at this brat! Since the day I've been taken ill he has not cared to come to me even once. As if he is not my son."

I was cut to the quick and kept thinking all day about what she had said. Had they really cheated Amma on that dark night? Maybe I had remained unconcerned about her illness because I was not her son. My elder sister, Bhaiya and Sabira looked so woebegone and worried over Amma all the time. They made such a fuss trying to force the medicine down her throat. But I felt that she was not really ill, that she was just putting on an act and wondered how long she would continue with this game.

Amma was annoyed with me. She said I was neglecting my studies, that I loafed about in the street. "Can't you stay in the house even for a minute?" she asked me testily. "Are there some relatives of yours out in the street that you must keep hobnobbing with them?"

So astounded was I at Amma's tantrum that the cricket ball I was holding slipped out of my hand. What did Amma mean by this jibe? Had she still a sneaking fear that one day I would disappear and join my real family?

I did not eat for two days. I lay in bed all the time and sulked. Amma thought I was ill. "Why don't you go out and play?" she would ask me. "Or do your homework."

Everyone in the house, while passing my bed, made it a point to dole out a lavish dose of Dos and Don'ts to me.

While supervising my studies, Abba used to say that if I did not understand some problem I would do well to tackle it bit by bit. "Spread it out thin and then attack it." But the questions that were tormenting me had spread themselves out too thinly for my liking. They had reached the point of engulfing my whole mind. I was getting scared.

At last they all decided I had become quite mad. One day my elder sister complained to Abba. "Abba, Amir does not do his homework. He just sits there with a book lying before him, constantly staring into the distance."

"We have never had a dolt in our family," Abba replied, angrily. "If Amir has taken it into his head to become a rickshawala, there's nothing I can do about it." Abba had said "in our family." In other words, it meant my father's family was distinct from my family. The thought distressed me.

When I came to think about it, it struck me that I was much fairer than my father. Abba, in fact, had a very dark complexion. In my childhood, when Abba used to hold me in his lap, his sister used to tease him. "Bhaiya," she would say, "a fair child in your lap looks so odd—almost an incongruity. People will think that you have stolen him." I would immediately get down from Abba's lap, as if he were a stranger to me. My brothers and sisters tried to keep me at arm's length. Sometimes they went into a huddle, whispering among themselves, as if they knew my story. At night, if there was a knock on the door, I would sit up in bed, looking flustered, fearing that someone had at last come to fetch me, foundling that I was. I would wipe my nose against Amma's rough kurta and start crying. And, "Here, show me the light!" Amma would cry. "I must make sure that this is Amir and none else." They would switch on the light. Holding me away from her she would scrutinize me intently. "No, no, this crying child cannot be mine. Can a lost child ever be found?" She would resignedly place her hand on my head. "Poor child!"

My childhood fears had not left me at all.

"What's the matter with you?" Amma suddenly woke up and slid closer to me, rubbing her eyes. "Why are you trembling?"

"Amma, Amir is frightened," Sabira cast a worried look at me. "He fears that someone is going to carry him off."

"Will anyone dare to while I am here?" Amma squeezed me against her and fondled my head.

"No, I must go." I brushed aside Amma's hand.

"Where will you go? And with whom?" Amma asked me in surprise. Where? With whom? The whole night these questions kept ringing in my ears.

It is well nigh impossible to trace a lost child without seeking somebody's help. And what made it almost a superhuman task in my case was that I had to trace my own self. . . . I had to look for myself among playing children, in running buses and speeding trains.

One day I saw a woman beating a small child as she dragged him along on the road. "Why are you so cruel—beating a child so mercilessly?" a passing woman admonished her. "Is he not your child?" Somewhere, a child who had been handed to an unknown woman in my place would also be beaten by that woman who was supposedly his mother. Why do women beat other mothers' children so mercilessly? Even my own mother, when she is annoyed with me, almost loses her head. Perhaps she is angry with me for having come to stay in her house.

When I was lost to my mother I became two persons instead of one. One part of me belonged to Amma and the other constituted that particular child who was sitting on the berth of a train compartment, watching the world go by in order to find a familiar face among those unknown persons. When will I discover the real "I?" When will the two "me"s merge into one?

I walked up and down the balcony of my house for hours together, hoping that someone would suddenly drop out of the blue and ask me how I happened to be here and maybe say, "Go back and join your kith and kin."

But I suffered the ordeal in solitary isolation. Nobody came to my rescue. The other "me" must also be passing through the same ordeal, I thought, cast adrift without any moorings. Far away from home, he must be sleeping on the bench of a train compartment which hurtles along endlessly without reaching anywhere. The black locomotive will pull the train through dark tunnels, dense forests and terrifying mountain ranges.

I often dreamed that I uprooted the vast network of railway tracks, bringing the trains all over the world to a standstill. And yet, that fool of a child kept sleeping on the train. Why doesn't someone wake him up? "Wake up, boy! Run home."

One day I came across an announcement in the newspaper. It said, "Athar, where are you? Return home at once. Your mother misses you. Her condition is serious. Nobody will reprimand you."

This advertisement was meant for me! I read it again and again and set out in search of the given address.

I knocked on the door of the house mentioned in the address. "Have you lost a child?" I asked.

They looked bewildered at my torn and shabby clothes, at my bleeding feet and my dust-smeared face.

"A mad boy! Keep out of his way." A small girl struck the warning note and quickly closed the window of the house.

I turned away, utterly disappointed.

Then I saw a boy coming in my direction. He was the same age as me and looked sad and frightened. He gave me a quick glance as if trying to recognize me. "Stop!" I said.

He stopped.

"Were the people in the house waiting for me?" I asked and held the announcement before him to read.

"Who are you?" he asked, looking up from the newspaper.

"They have all refused to recognize me. But I've a hunch that my near and dear ones are waiting for my return. They are sure to recognize me the moment they set eyes on me."

"Stop telling lies," the young boy exploded in anger. "This announcement relates to me, I'm the prodigal returning home."

He looked at me with suspicious eyes.

"So you are the one who has uprooted all the railway tracks?" I asked in a cheerful voice. "So you've woken up from your sleep at last?"

"But who are you?" He gave me an intense look.

The old rigmarole had started again. I stood there thinking for some time and then jumped with joy.

"Now I know," I said. "You are you and I am I." I again jumped with joy. "We have been restored to our respective homes."

I broke into a run, delirious with joy. I kicked at the stones lying on the way. Stepping away just in time from racing cycles and speeding cars to avoid colliding with them, and parrying the stones that were hurled at me by naughty children, I just ran on, happy at the thought that at last even those heartless children had recognized who I was.

"There goes a lunatic!" the people of the mohalla cried.

Yes, all of them had recognized me. Now even my mother would have no difficulty in recognizing me. So, "I" at last had been found. It had been a long and frustrating journey and I had returned home dead with fatigue. But I could see them from a distance. They were watching me with curious eyes, eyes full of compassion and deep concern for me.

They caught me in time from falling down.

"Your son has returned!" they cried. "Look at the state he is in!"

They pushed me into Amma's outstretched arms.

"Allah, it's indeed my Amir!"

She held my face between her hands. She looked at it, puzzled.

My heart was suddenly empty, as if all the joy had suddenly gone out of it. Disconsolate, I pushed Amma away.

I am yet to discover who "I" am.

THAYYAAL

Rupavati

Translated by Geeta Dharmarajan

"They want nothing. No jewels. No gold. Nothing. They won't ask you to spend one paisa on your girl's marriage. What do you say?"

The coffee he has just poured into his mouth spills on to his bare chest, but does Muthiah care? He looks at the old woman, stares at her, forgetting to gulp down the coffee that is there in his mouth.

A toothless grin spreads over the old woman's face. She is sitting, her old legs stretched out before her, her back resting against the wall. Her long heavy gold earrings, the thandatti, dangle. They catch the fire of the sun.

Children scream and play somewhere inside the house. Alongside one wall of the open courtyard lie many bags of grain, stacked in three rows, each as tall as two men standing one on top of the other. Like gold dust, grain lies scattered on the floor. Wherever you look, signs of prosperity are visible.

Just that morning, Muthiah had seriously started the search for a groom for his daughter. She had reached marriageable age. He would be able to keep her home no longer. Tongues would wag. . . . He had heard that Ponnazhaghu was looking for a bride for his son who worked in Karaikudi and had hastened to his house, not even pausing to eat a full breakfast. And Ponnazhaghu had not been home. Muthiah had found him out in the auction house, leaning on the wheel of a sugarcane cart, and, what did he want?

"Thirty sovereigns of gold . . . "

Muthiah wiped his face and neck with his towel . . .

"Three thousand rupees in hand . . . "

Muthiah, as if his legs could bear his weight no more, had leaned against the cart too . . .

"Dowry items should be worth not less than ten thousand rupees . . . "

Without a by-your-leave, Muthiah had moved away . . .

"Appu . . . Appu!" called Ponnazhaghu, but Muthiah had slung his towel on his bare shoulders and just walked on.

Muthiah's first son is in the army. Lives with his family in some distant corner of North India. The result of his marriage—a mortgaged house. The second son is a fitter in a city company. Muthiah had borrowed on his lands for this son's marriage. The sons, of course, quite religiously paid back the interest every month. But, the principal? When Muthiah had gone to the bank again, thinking he could take one more loan with the same surety. He found out that he would be able to raise no more than two thousand rupees. Of what use was that?

The income from his field was enough for the repayments of loan on his field and for feeding the three mouths at home. Their two, three cows of local breed yielded enough money, under his wife's persistent coaxing, for her to join a monthly chit fund in order to buy some stainless steel utensils for their daughter's dowry. This also, when the need arose, took care of small expenses, unexpected emergencies.

Muthiah lay down in the garden house in the park. The evening mantharai, the night-blooming arali, impressed upon his mind's eye. His anguish slowly lessened.

When he reached home, his wife Kunjaram was getting ready to milk the cows. She had tied the hind legs of the first one tightly together. She had got the saliva-dribbling calf away from the swollen teats of its mother and had tied it up too.

She saw Muthiah. "Oh, you have come! Where were you all this while?"

What had he achieved that he could give her an answer?

"After you left, the old mother from the Big House had sent for you. Aatha's man has been back and forth, back and forth, three times already."

Milk hit the vessel sharply.

"What does she want? I can't think why. . . . Well, let me go see."

"Wait. I'll make you some coffee first."

The old woman is very wealthy, a millionaire. Sons, daughters, grandchildren, she has many. To Muthiah she seems as full and spread-out as a banyan tree. She was widowed a year ago. She is a distant relation of his. For functions and mournings they send word to him. Muthiah too visits them on occasions such as these. The old woman always seems to have a special affection for him.

Why had she called? What could be so urgent that a messenger should come three times in search of him? Thoughts running pell-mell within him, he took time only to wash his face before he hurried to her. The paved road would take time. A short cut?

Muthiah stepped out of his house through the back door. He walked briskly, along the winding narrow path between two fields, dense with undergrowth, overgrown with wild bushes . . .

Thayyaal walked, a basket full of garbage resting lightly on her head.

She had the heart-stopping loveliness of a sixteen year old.

Height, taller than the average girl.

Color, the burnished gold of young mango leaves.

Her sari rode jauntily over the tender softness of young ankles to reveal feet good enough to be eaten.

Her hair, thick and glowing black, a cascade that would reach to well below a slender waist, was now pulled back and rudely shoved into a knot.

Bare under her sari, her firm rounded breasts stuck out of the folds, moved in rhythm as she walked, seemed to want to tear out of the restrictions of the breast cage.

In preparation for the heavy thandatti, the earrings she would have to wear after she was married, she had screws of cane in the holes in her earlobes and the cane would get thicker as the holes grew.

Her nose, a connoisseur's delight.

Her lips, full. Tempting.

Hers was the unselfconscious beauty that made young hearts throb.

Hers was a beauty that rose unbidden behind closed eyelids. She was the heavenly goddess of Thenmaapattu village.

Daily, at dusk, she would collect the cow-dropping, leaves and grass from the cow-pen and take them to the fields. It was something all the young women of the village did, and no great burden for her anyway.

She changed hands to support the basket on her head. The movement made the sari slide off her right bosom. It fell into the valley between her breasts.

A cool breeze touched her skin, flirted with it.

Bold in the knowledge that there was no one around, she did not think it necessary to cover herself.

He had reached the spot before Thayyaal got there . . .

Waiting for her to reach there . . .

Walking swiftly along the path that abuts on the village, and then slinking under the spreading tamarind tree, to watch, to wait, to look . . .

As she came, closer . . . closer . . .

Descending into the gentle slope to hide . . .

Burying himself into the lush undergrowth that sprawled onto the slender pathway . . .

Staring with drunken eyes . . .

Staring, staring, Chandiyar Vellaisami watched her beauty, his eyes ready to fall out of their sockets, his mouth hanging open . . .

"What is this, Ayyah? I have been asking you for the past few minutes and you just sit there, not saying anything?"

Muthiah quickly swallows the coffee.

"Oh, nothing, Aatha," he begins to say, hesitantly. "When someone says he wants no dowry when asking for the hand of a girl in marriage, I wonder if something is wrong with the boy and . . . "

"Oh, you idiot of a man! You know my younger brother, don't you?"

"Chokkan!"

The thandatti shake to indicate a No.

"Muthukaruppan!"

"His elder son is in Madurai, as you know . . . "

"In the collector's office!"

"Yes, Rajangham. I ask your daughter's hand for him."

The happiness that had started spreading through him, at the beginning of this conversation, disappears like a bubble.

"For his status, his wealth. . . . Me . . . my . . . "

"As soon as your wife Kunjaram gave birth to a girl, I had decided that she would come to our house as a bride."

"Does your brother agree?"

"He was here this morning. Waited for you till now. He has just left."

In Muthiah's heart a fullness grows, a happiness dances within.

"Here, Chegappi, bring those things."

The old woman's daughter-in-law, who has come into the inner courtyard on some work, now withdraws into a side room.

Unaware that two victorious gloating eyes were enjoying her every movement from within the bushes, Thayyaal walked into the fields.

His veins ached when he saw the gentle movement of her back, the swell of her thighs under the sari.

She turned the basket upside down.

The fields were quiet and serene, languishing in the after-heat like a woman who has just given birth.

Thayyaal sighed. She shook the end of her sari off her head where, till now, it had served as a support for the basket. She wiped her neck and face and the sweat that dribbled between her breasts.

"Aaa . . . ha!"

Clicking fingers, he jumped. He trembled and twitched with impatience.

Arranging her sari to cover her modesty again, Thayyaal picked the basket from the ground.

He who had watched her every movement with fire in his loins was all set to feed on her, lust and drunkenness reaching their respective peaks. And when she walked past him . . . like lightning Chandiyar jumped on to her path. He grabbed the basket in her hands.

"Ayyyoooo!" A cry of alarm rose from her. Startled, she pushed herself away from him. Her eyes filled with fear, the numbing fright of animals. Her basket fell. It rolled down the slope.

Chandiyar caught her with both his hands . . .

The large tray is meticulously arranged. There are full coconuts on its fringes, bunches of bananas. In the middle are a silk sari, a silk blouse bit, a silk-edged dhoti, and a towel. On this is a stack of rupees. And, balancing on top, are the auspicious turmeric roots, fresh and green-yellow.

Slowly, resting her weight on the palm that is pressed against the floor, the old woman gets up, leaning on her daughter-in-law for support. She takes the tray and holds it out to Muthiah.

"For me. . . ?" He gapes. He quickly gets up from where he's sitting on the ground. "Is all this for me? I don't understand . . . "

The old woman laughs like a child, her heart brimming over with love.

"Cheee! Let go!"

With sudden swiftness the situation was clear to Thayyaal. Like a hunted deer she tried to flee.

Chandiyar Vellaisami bounded forward and snatched the end of the sari that lay on the ground.

He wrapped this round his wrist. He clapped his hands and laughed. He started pulling her towards him.

Panting, one hand covering her breasts, Thayyaal used the other hand to pull her sari towards her.

"I warn you . . . let go! When my father comes to know, he will skin you alive!"

Thayyaal pushed aside the need to cry that welled up inside her.

"What do I care what happens after now, dee? Now, all I need is you." He slobbered.

"Chee! You drunken dog! Let go!"

She pulled at the sari.

Slowly, deliberately, enjoying every moment, he gathered her sari, pulling her along with it.

There was nothing she could do.

Then, in a flash, she pirouetted. Leaving the sari in its entirety in his hands, she fled, Thayyaal.

With three yards of the sari in his hands, the other three on the ground, Vellaisami growled at the sudden emptiness . . .

He flung the sari to the ground.

"Where will you run, you?" he snarled. "I am a drunkard, am I? You won't marry me, will you? Well, we'll see, we'll see. We have to decide one way or the other today, or my name is not Vellaisami . . . "

Fingering his handsome moustache, he proceeded to examine each and every bush.

He pulled apart bushes, his hands unsteady, shaking with anger.

A thorn pricked. His anger spilled over.

"Oh God . . . God . . . please, please . . . "

He was searching in the bush opposite hers.

She froze.

She called on every god she knew.

And from above her head, a call from the branches of the tamarind tree. "Chillambane . . . Karuppane . . . Bhumatha. . . . I have knocked down all the tamarind fruits. Come pick them up!"

It broke the silence of the forest.

Like a hurt snake, Vellaisami shivered.

He looked up.

The blue sky. The small somber leaves of the tamarind tree. The fan-spread of the tall palm. They twirled and swam like a merry-go-round in his eyes.

Who, who was up there? One . . . or many?

Swearing profusely, "Ai! Who's that?" screamed Vellaisami.

"It's me."

A ghostly, oracle-like voice.

"Ai, you! What are you doing there?"

"I am shaking the tamarind tree. Bhumatha! There are lots of tamarind fruits in the pond. Pick them, too!"

Chala . . . Chala . . . Chala . . .

The adjoining tamarind tree shook and jumped like a ghoul. Like a flurry of shooting stars came the tamarind fruits.

"Ah . . . hath . . . thu!" Vellaisami spat out a thick glob of saliva. Venom. . . . The bastards had spoiled his game!

He peered at the surrounding bushes. He mumbled, "Okay, so you have got the better of me today. But just you wait, wait. Where can you go, after all?"

He swore. He slowly walked towards the village.

As soon as Vellaisami disappeared, two coffee-brown legs shimmied down the trunk of the tamarind tree and jumped off its lowest branch. Slip-sliding down the slope, he picked up the sari.

"Aatha! Aatha! Sister, sister!"

"I am here!"

From a bush, an arm appeared. It took the sari.

Some seconds . . . Thayyaal emerged hastily, tucking the sari at her waist.

She could not believe her eyes. Before her stood a tassel-headed, naked, eight year old.

Tears welled. They dripped from the sides of her eyes. She bent down, took his hands in hers, raised them to her eyes . . . to press them reverently in thanksgiving.

"I can never forget this, Aatha," says Muthiah.

Words slide into each other, their edges touched with emotion.

The old woman frees her hands. Taking the bag that her daughter-in-law holds, she takes all the things from the tray and puts them in.

When she picks the paper currency, Muthiah is astonished once again. How much money! At least five thousand rupees there! The silk would have cost not a paisa less than a thousand. Is the old woman mad?

"If your brother is going to be spending on everything for the wedding, then why this sari, this money . . . "

The smile fades from the old woman's face. Her mind seems to wander. "Do you not remember that day, many years ago?" she asks. "Of course, then you were a small boy, curly-haired, eight years old . . . "

What can Muthiah say?

"The very next month I got married. He was rich. I told my husband then that I wanted to give my share of the family money to you. A young lad may not know what to do with it, he said and, taking the money, he went that same day and put it in the bank. Let him marry, have a daughter, you can give it to him then, he said. That money has also grown and branched, like me," says the old woman, Thayyaal.

Just a Simple Bridge

Rajee Seth

Translated by Jai Ratan

For three days Tilak Raj had been running around, trying to buy a room cooler. Tilak Raj's quest was touched with a sense of urgency. There had been a letter from his son in America. He was coming home. It was just a midsummer break, but there was no point in wasting those four weeks, Ladi had written. And, anyway, he'd prefer to spend the time at home with his people, he had said.

The trip would cost his son a lot of money—nothing less than ten thousand rupees. It seemed inconceivably extravagant, but Tilak Raj had decided not to worry about that. The money would go from his son's pocket, not his own. To think that his son had such money to spend just to come home on holiday would normally have made him hold his head high with pride. Yet, he found his stomach churning at the thought of so much money being spent so heedlessly. Ten thousand rupees was what Tilak Raj earned in a whole year—and he spent it all on maintaining the family. Couldn't his son forgo his holiday and save the money?

But it was futile to think in that vein. The money was not his; it was not even his son's to save. It was earmarked for his air passage home. If he did not avail himself of it, he would lose it anyway, by default, Ladi had explained in one of his letters. Such expenditures were known as "actuals." There was no question of making a saving on them. His son's letters were full of snippets of information. They conjured up visions of wide roads, dazzling lights, comfortable homes—of cornucopia. Ladi had said it was all different there. He wrote, "Papa, you can't imagine what it's really like, being here . . . " and, grudgingly, Tilak Raj would murmur that maybe Ladi was right, that imagination did have a way of distorting reality. But then, a country where they gave away thousands of rupees for just a holiday at home. . . ?

Tilak Raj felt guilty, thinking in this strain. Didn't he want his son to come home on this visit? Was he not equating his son with money? What if his son guessed his thoughts? Although he was sitting alone in his room, he shrank into himself, as if everyone could see the workings of his mind.

Did Ladi remember any of the things his father had told him so many times as he was growing up? Money was not everything, Tilak Raj believed. "Look at me," he would tell Ladi, "my whole life lies before you like an open book. Hardship is the best teacher in life; undergo hardships and you make good in life. You are still a young boy and your whole life lies before you. At your age, I used to carry a sack weighing a mound and a half on my back . . . " The fact that every morning, while rolling up his sleeves to fetch bucketfuls of water from the tap, Tilak Raj caught himself looking wistfully at his thin arms, didn't change anything.

Tilak Raj gave himself a mental shake. At his age why was he getting entangled in such morbid thoughts? What was past was past. True, he may not get a paisa from his son, but then, he was not so badly off. Both his daughters were married. One of them was happy, the other a little less happy—but he'd never allowed his thoughts to dwell on his second daughter. By now he had learned the knack of keeping his mind only on those thoughts that did not disturb him. At night, while lying by his side, his wife would complain about their second daughter's lot, and, without even thinking he would turn on his side and remark sharply, "One must learn to take the rough with the smooth. Take your own case. Have you been happy in every possible way? Did you get all that you aspired for in life?"

"Are you listening?" he now asked his wife as he ate his evening meal. "Ladi is coming. I'm thinking of buying a cooler."

His wife's eyes widened. "What?" she asked. "A cooler?"

"He must have acquired new habits. He will be here just for a few days and may not be able to stand the searing lu. You know how it is these days."

"So what! He knows all about the hot winds. Surely, he couldn't have taken so soon to lordly ways. His university gives him a stipend only to acquire higher education."

Tilak Raj was annoyed. This woman would never understand. A woman who cooked one meal and saved something from it for the next and then, on top of it, wanted to be patted on her back for it, would never understand. She was the kind of woman who gloated over the fact that she could cook a pumpkin and make an extra curry from its rind.

Next day, he left the house earlier than usual, fearing that he would not have enough time that evening for his shopping. Moreover, in the evening the shopkeepers became too weary to treat customers with the same effusiveness. They sized up each customer from his dress and modulated their tone accordingly. They were also always in a hurry to reach home. Tilak Raj found it easier to plan his day to suit the shopkeepers' moods, to give in to the pressures of a situation. He had been doing so all his life.

The shopkeeper had just rolled up his shutters and here was the first customer of the day! It augured well. "Yes, what can I do for you?" he asked Tilak Raj, in a voice laced with honey.

"I want to buy a cooler."

"Oh, yes. Oh, yes." The shopkeeper pulled out a drawer and took out a thick wad of papers. "Zenith. Coolex. Summer Time Supreme. We have them all. Here's the price-list. From eighteen hundred upwards. This one is very sophisticated. The latest model. The pump . . . "

Tilak Raj was lost in thought. At last, "Can I hire a cooler? I mean for one season?"

"But why not buy one, sa'ab? In four seasons you can realize the cost of the cooler."

"Well . . . "

Without soiling his hand by shoving it into the sack, the shopkeeper seemed to have gauged the quality of its content. With measured coolness he said, "Yes, coolers are available for hire, but we don't stock such things. Try the fourth shop in this row."

Tilak Raj felt as if a rough piece of rope that was grating against his neck had been removed. He came out of the shop with great alacrity and walked away. His toes hurt as they usually did when he walked too fast. But the pain would have to subside of its own accord. His son was coming on a visit. He pushed his chest out, although he found the effort a bit taxing at his age.

Tilak Raj's wife eyed the cooler doubtfully as it was unloaded from the cart and deposited outside her door in the glaring afternoon heat. "Why have you brought it here?"

"Isn't this Government Quarter Number S-75?"

"Yes, so it is."

"Then it is meant for this house, Sa'ab is following."

Like a child with a new toy in her hands, she turned over the word "Sa'ab" in her mind. The pigeon that was lodged in her heart and which had stayed still for such a long time, suddenly fluttered its wings. "Sa'ab must have told you where the cooler is to be installed."

The workers who had sat down on the ground to rest did not consider it necessary to reply to her question. Taking their angochhas from their shoulders they started fanning themselves.

She went in and came out with cold water from the surahi. "Here, drink it," she said. "Should I add some sugar to it?"

Just then Tilak Raj, whom the laborers had called Sa'ab, came into view—his face glistening with sweat, his shirt and black terylene pants showing damp patches. The cooler was installed in the window opening on to the narrow veranda. The electrician left, and husband and wife planted themselves in front of the cooler. A blast of cool air flew past their bodies. Not that they had not experienced a cooler before but now, they were overwhelmed by its comforting presence in their own house. They could manipulate the weather just by touching an electric switch!

"Shall I switch it off?" his wife asked. "What a humming noise it makes. Must be consuming a lot of electricity."

"Keep it on for some time. Today at least. We won't use it again until Ladi comes."

She saw that her husband himself was not showing any sign of moving away from the cooler. He had taken off his sweat-drenched banian.

She cut two big chunks from the watermelon she had left overnight in the bucket to cool off. They ate, forgetting to switch off the cooler.

In the days that followed, they often dusted the cooler, checked its reserve of water but never got round to switching it on. Tilak Raj sometimes reminded his wife that whether she used it or not they would have to pay the full season's rent for it—six hundred rupees, not a rupee less.

"But then the electricity bill?" his wife murmured and they continued to sweat.

Such luxuries were distant dreams for them, even though they were probably part of their son's lifestyle. "It demands a formal inauguration," decided Tilak Raj's wife. They would spring it as a surprise on the boy. He had gone far by virtue of his own enterprise; his father had nothing to do with it. And now, he was coming back from a cold country and it would not behoove his parents to plunge him into a furnace. He was coming out of consideration for his parents. But for them, he could have spent his holidays in a more enjoyable manner.

The day before Ladi was to arrive, Tilak Raj tried—in his timid way—to ask Mr. Khosla at his office if he could drive him to the airport in his car to receive his son.

Mr. Khosla stared at Tilak Raj. The fool! He didn't even know the proper decorum of making a request. What was so special about a son going abroad for education? While making a request should one forget one's humble origins?

"You know I drive the car myself . . . and at the ungodly hour of three in the morning?" Mr. Khosla said.

"No, no, of course not," Tilak Raj murmured hastily, humiliated by the look on Mr. Khosla's face.

And Ladi came home on his own.

Tilak Raj restrained himself. He didn't know how to show the surge of happiness he felt at seeing Ladi, who looked suave, at ease, happy. Ladi's complexion had improved and his mother felt his muscles had become more prominent as she swayed in visible happiness in his arms. When Ladi bent down to touch his father's feet, blood coursed through Tilak Raj's old body. He gently patted Ladi's head and then stood back. He didn't know what to do next. His son seemed an unknown commodity, an alien.

When Ladi had lived at home, Tilak Raj had not paid him much heed. The boy had gone his own way while he himself went about his daily pursuits like an oil crusher's blinkered bullock, round and round, leaving home in the morning, returning each evening. A victim of chronic constipation, a good part of every morning had always been spent cajoling his bowels. Then there was the rush of getting to the bus stop in time so that he could be at the head of the long queue of passengers and, once in the office, there was the daily tension of maintaining his dignity as he hovered over the thin line separating him from the white-collared gentility. How often had he felt as if his superiors resented his head clerk's stature. He had come to the conclusion, quite early in his working life, that peace was not a commodity to be easily had by one torn between vicissitudes. Perhaps one could rest only after retirement from service, when the heat of one's blood had swallowed all life's longings and desires.

Ladi was plying him with questions touching upon his health, life in general and prospects of an advancement in his job.

Why didn't Ladi understand? Could things change in two years when they had not changed in the course of so many long years? Perhaps, having been away for so long, Ladi had forgotten the temper and tenor of the house.

"Will Saru and Nita be visiting us?" Ladi asked eagerly.

"Yes, your sisters will come when it suits their convenience," Ladi's mother said. The words implied that if she invited her daughters she would have to bear their travel expenses from Bangalore and Lucknow. And this year her financial position had been undermined due to sundry unforeseen expenses to which had been added the burden of hiring a cooler.

But, it didn't seem as if Ladi had understood. He was going around the small house, taking in everything with a casual glance. He looked behind the curtains made from discarded saris, at the cement shelves built into the walls. He went to the back of the house and examined the small kitchen garden. He stood there gazing at the blazing sun, remembering how, long ago, his mother used to describe it as "the angry demon raining down fire."

His mother urged him to come inside, tacitly reminding him that he still had to have his bath and meal. They reminded him that he must be feeling worn-out after his twenty-two hour sleepless journey, sitting stiff and tied down to his narrow seat. She offered him a glass of cool panna.

"Ah," said Ladi with pleasure. "Rivers of milk and juice flow there. But this raw mango juice laced with green mint leaves . . . oh, it's divine! We never get it there."

He playfully squeezed his mother's knees.

His mother beamed at him. But Tilak Raj, sitting nearby, had nothing to say. He felt uncertain and strange. How difficult it was to make even a simple bridge between a knee and a pair of hands!

Then, a feeling buried under the debris of time suddenly erupted and lodged itself in his throat. In spite of his son's No, no! he poured the panna from his glass into his son's.

What more could he do?

The meal over, it was time for the afternoon siesta. Curtains were drawn against the glare outside, and the whirring of the cooler filled the house. The hot winds of summer, the lu, were held at bay, like unwelcome guests.

The couple waited expectantly for Ladi to say something about the cooler. Now it was too big a presence to ignore.

Ladi's mother remembered how, as a young boy, when Ladi sat down to study, she would wet a straw hand fan and keep fanning him. When she dozed off, resting her back against the wall, "Ma, the ceiling fan . . . " Ladi would say and, "No, son, it makes the room so hot. A hand fan is better. We can at least wet it," she would reply and start fanning him with renewed vigor. Did he not remember?

But Ladi only said, "I had planned my journey in such a way so that I would arrive on a Sunday. I knew Papa would be home and we could have a nice time together."

"Oh yes," Tilak Raj murmured, but it was obvious that he had not heard the words that would have touched his heart.

Yes, Tilak Raj's mind had wandered. He couldn't help but feel proud that now, finally, he had done something special for his son. He felt he was standing at the other end of what constituted give and take. But, words failed him. Even if he could put his thoughts into words, it would only sound cheap, mean. It would be akin to plunging a knife into his skin just to show off the color of his blood.

Ladi was stretched out on the cot over which his mother had spread a milk-white bedsheet, with a brand new pillowcase for the pillow. He made some noises when his father lay down on a mat spread on the floor, but soon reconciled himself.

"I was hoping Barre Bhaiya would already be here."

"I thought I would send your elder brother word on your arrival," Ladi's mother said. "He comes only when he is in a mood for it. For that matter, over the years we have given up hope of . . . "

"Ma, everybody has some limitations."

"Maybe, maybe not," Tilak Raj said. "There must be something lacking in us."

A silence hung in the air. They all seemed to have withdrawn into their shells. Tilak Raj wondered if Ladi was indulgent to them now because they were no longer a part of his life? He had traveled far, learned much, lived the life of a grown-up man with problems that they could not even begin to imagine. How could his parents span the chasm?

Tilak Raj shook his head. He sighed. But the next moment he realized that there was no need to agonize over these questions. Ladi had come home to relax, sleep and have a peaceful time. And now Ladi was asleep. Why should he brood over these matters? People came and people went. And time too, went its own way.

It was close to seven when Ladi awoke. The evening sun of May was still relentless.

Seeing him stir, his mother asked, "Tea? Milkshake? What do you generally prefer in the evening?"

Ladi laughed as he got off his bed. "My favorite drink?" He playfully pinched his mother's arm. "Don't you know my habits, Ma? Did I go abroad to study or. . . ?"

Sipping his tea, he asked, "Does Keshav ever visit us?"

"Yes, once in a blue moon."

"And Seema?"

"She drops in often while returning from college."

"I'll visit them today. It's been such a long tine since I have walked under such a bright sun. You emerge from an air-conditioned room and walk into another air-conditioned room there!"

"You'll find it very hot."

"No, I won't. And I won't mind even if I do. I'll have a bath on my return when I'm all drenched in sweat. People over there do not know what great fun that is!"

Tilak Raj suddenly felt apprehensive, as if as soon as Ladi stepped out of the house its walls would crumble and fall.

But then, what did he want? Why was he obsessed with this thought of asking Ladi if he had seen something new in the house? He thought Ladi should know the specific reason why he had bought the cooler this summer. How he had to demean himself to buy it. No, he told himself, not he but Ladi's mother was sure to broach the subject. While she was talking he would lie there with closed eyes and quietly, without interrupting, pretending to be asleep, he would listen to the goings-on between mother and son. Lying there he would listen to the sound of his bridge being built from the other end, he'd listen to his wife saying, "He has done all this for you . . . only for you. Otherwise, as you know, all his life he has suffered only because he is so willful. He is always so unbending."

Tilak Raj heard his wife say, "Your tea is getting cold. I've told you so many times I've brought your tea!"

He was still lying on the mat with his eyes closed. As he opened them it seemed as if inside him, other eyes opened too.

He sat up on his mat.

Ladi was taking off his tight, striped shirt.

"Today I must change into my white kurta." He was pulling his suitcase from under the cot.

"Arre, it still looks brand new! Don't you ever wear it there?"

"No, Ma, machine-washing is so expensive there. It can spell my financial ruin. So the kurta just stayed in my trunk."

He smiled wryly at his mother, then went to wash his face at the wash basin in the veranda. "It's still very hot outside," he said, coming back into the room. "No?"

Tilak Raj's ears perked up.

Ladi had started singing a film tune under his breath. Standing in the middle of the room, he had pulled down his trousers from under the towel which was still dangling from above his waist. Kicking off the trousers, he pulled white pajamas over his legs. Then he whipped the towel off his waist and hitched up the pajamas and knotted the pajama cord. He put on his kurta and went and sat in the chair which his father had bought at a private furniture auction at his office.

Cool breeze from the cooler wafted past him.

Tilak Raj saw that his wife was totally absorbed in her son.

"It's so calm and quiet here. We don't have such peaceful evenings over there," Ladi said cheerfully as he got up from the chair and went to comb his hair, wetting the comb as was his habit.

His father raised his eyes to the old-looking mirror hanging from the wall. Would Ladi not notice the cooler reflected there?

"I may be late, Ma."

"But you'll be back for your dinner, won't you?"

"Yes, I may. But I can't be sure."

"I don't mind it. But, your father will miss you at dinner. You know how he has hired a . . . er . . . er . . . "

Tilak Raj mumbled and pressed his wife's toe with his foot.

"Okay then," said Ladi promptly. "I'm in no hurry. I'll go visiting tomorrow and make it a leisurely affair. In a short while we shall pull out our cots and sit in the open."

"No, go. It's all right with us," Tilak Raj said, his voice subdued. He could not understand why his son had failed to notice the new in the house, mark it from the old, why he could not see the huge contraption fitted into the window which was releasing such blasts of cool breeze at such breathtaking speed? Didn't he remember that it had not been there before?

Tilak Raj felt a sort of heaviness steal over him.

Tilak Raj watched his son walk out of the front door.

He switched off the cooler and returned to the mat on the floor. It didn't matter, he told himself sternly. He would not think about himself. He would concentrate on his son and his son's achievements. He would think only of Ladi. Just that, and nothing more.

It was better that way.

I Am Complete

Varsha Das

Translated by the author

Today, when the judge, sitting on a high chair and wearing a black robe, announces that I am free, I feel as if two wings are growing on my shoulders.

I feel like flying.

Or like somersaulting in the open sky.

Or, why don't I go and sit on the topmost branches of the innumerable trees around here?

Where should I build my nest? On a gulmohar tree? Or on a mango tree? A neem would be cooler, but isn't a banyan tree more dependable?

Or . . . why don't I enjoy each one for a while? Then I will be able to experience the comforts and security each has to offer.

But then, wouldn't I exhaust my entire life collecting experiences with no time left to build a nest anywhere?

Is it necessary to build a nest? I have not taken any vow to build my own nest with straws collected by me alone. So many birds have invited me to share their nests with them. And not just crows and kites. One is a peacock and the other a pigeon. There is an eagle, and a parrot too.

The choice is mine!

At this moment, I am sitting on the tender branch of a drumstick tree. The whole tree is adorned with white flowers. It looks happy, almost as if it is drunk with the feeling. I, too, am infected by its intoxication.

But here comes a cool and bitter-smelling breeze from the neem tree. Its light slap drives away my drunkenness.

My wings become smaller and smaller and smaller. They disappear.

I am not a bird, but a human being. Not just a human being, a woman. Not just a woman, but Kanupriya. Tornadoes have not yet been able to raze me. Jabbed and pricked by many thorns, I have still not become thick-skinned.

From a small pin-prick, blood oozes out of me. From a faint touch of Kanu's kiss, gliding on airy waves from a distant land, my cheeks blush!

Kanu is my love, my life. After receiving my freedom, I wanted to build a house with Kanu. But that, too, did not work. We too were separated, perhaps forever. Still, the moment his voice reaches me through the enlarged circles of sound waves, my body gets charged. I feel his touch then. And the river starts flowing. It is not a playful bouncing river, but a deep and calm one.

As we had strolled in the Tirumal hills, Kanu's hand in mine, we had both felt that two young streams had hugged each other. These streams together were to turn into a river that had dreamed of making a house in the sea. But nothing like that happened. Kanu and I started living on two different planets and the distance between us was of very many light years, a distance so great that today, when those wings grew on me, not even for a moment did I feel like visiting Kanu. And still, the experience of love is as fresh as ever, as if it had happened only a moment ago!

When we were both young vigorous streams, Kanu had said, "Look at the velocity of our love. No force on earth can obstruct it."

Then I had said, "But suppose we encounter a huge mountain on the way!"

He replied, "We shall divide and again unite on the other side."

We did encounter a mountain. We did divide, but did not unite afterwards. On reaching the other side of the mountain, I waited for him, but he took a different path! When I saw him veer away, for a moment I felt the ground was slipping away from under me.

Fortunately, the very next moment, the sky started pouring its affection. The drizzle caressed me, soaked me in its motherly love and said, "This is good for you, and for him too. Had you merged again, the river would have been in spate and would have destroyed everything around it. Let him flow alone too. Let him be reminded of your love. Yes, he will definitely pretend that there was nobody called Priya ever in his life. This need for pretense is his great weakness. And self-centeredness is another. It is good that you have separated before your love turned to hatred."

And it stopped drizzling. I felt smooth, even ground under me. My mind and body were serene. I found a vast stretch of land before me. A free land. An endless land. I felt as if the whole Earth was mine. This sky, too. I am not alone. If I open my arms, I can embrace the whole universe.

I am complete.

Contributors

Jeelani Bano's involvement with writing short fiction began in 1955. So far eighteen of her books have been published, many of which have been highly acclaimed. Her works have been translated into other Indian and foreign languages, including English, French, and Russian. She has received the Ghalib Award, Doshiza Award, Sovietland-Nehru Award, and Nuqoosh Award, Lahore. Jeelani Bano has written for television as well, especially for women-based programs. Committed to the cause of equality for rural women, she has also been involved in development programs in rural areas of Andhra Pradesh. Some of her more prominent works include *Aiwan-e-Ghazal, Baarish-e-Sang, Jugnu Aur Sitarey, Roshni ke Minar, Nirvaan,* and *Paraya Ghar.*

Mahua Bhattacharya is a lecturer at Calcutta University and a translator. She has translated the autobiography of the filmmaker Joris Ivens from French into Bangla.

Rimli Bhattacharya is a comparatist by training. She taught English at Jawaharlal Nehru University for many years and is at present on fellowship from the Indian Council for Social Sciences Research.

Pradipta Borgohain has a Ph.D. from the University of Illinois at Urbana-Champaign and is a reader in English at Guwahati University. He writes for local and national newspapers and magazines, and has translated short stories and novels for various publishers. He also has two collections of sociological and literary articles, in Asomiya (Assamese), to his credit.

Asha Damle is a teacher, writer, and translator. She translates from Marathi into English. Among her publications are two collections of short stories, *Bhoomi* and *Kanya eka Swapnaleati,* and the novel *Bal Asawe Pankhat.*

Kamala Das publishes in English under her own name and in Malayalam under the pseudonym Madhavikutty. Born into a well-known literary family, she is one of the few women writers in the world to have handled so many literary genres with great success in two distinct languages—English and Malayalam. In addition to several novelettes and numerous short stories, she has published poems, children's

123

fiction, and an autobiography. She has also written scripts for television films, and does a regular column for a Malayalam weekly. Her poetry has been translated into several Indian and foreign languages. She has won the Asian Poetry Prize, the ASAN World Prize for poetry, the Kerala Sahitya Akademi Award for her short stories in Malayalam, and the Chimanlal Award for her fearless journalism.

VARSHA DAS has a Ph.D. in nonformal education. She has been writing and translating since she was sixteen years old. She is the author of one collection of short fiction and numerous books for children. She has been a resource person for the Asian Cultural Centre for UNESCO, Tokyo. Das has translated poems and short stories from Oriya, Bangla, Marathi, and English into Hindi, Gujarati, and English, and has written plays on art and education.

ANITA DESAI writes short stories and novels including books for children. Her novel *Fire on the Mountain* won the Royal Society of Literature's Winifred Holtby Memorial Prize and the 1978 Sahitya Akademi Award. She has been a member of the Advisory Board for English and of the American Academy of Arts and Letters, as well as a fellow of the Royal Society of Literature. She has worked as an educator at various American colleges and at Cambridge University. *Clear Light of Day* won her her first Booker nomination in 1980. Subsequently *In Custody* was nominated in 1984 and *Fasting, Feasting* in 1999.

ASHAPURNA DEVI, a prolific writer of short stories and novels, had taught herself to read. She wrote primarily at night after all her household chores were over. Her literary career spanned almost five decades. Her most popular novels were *Prathom Pratishruti, Subarnalata,* and *Bakulkatha.* She received the Jnanpith Award in 1976. It has been difficult to find the right English word for the title of her story. "Izzat" suggests something more than the dictionary meaning of "honor," "prestige," or "respect." Of Urdu origin, the word "izzat" is used extensively in northern India but class and gender infuse new and varying meanings and nuances into the speaker's usage. In this story, the world has more to do with "self-respect" than with "prestige."

MAHASWETA DEVI, an activist-writer who has carved a definite niche for herself, was awarded the Sahitya Akademi Award in 1979 and the Jnanpith Award in 1997. She has gone deeply into the question of written Bangla, and in her stories one often finds spoken Bangla sliding into the more formal written Bangla, with a sprinkling of English words. She has many novels, collections of stories, books for children, and plays to her credit. She has also coauthored, in Hindi, *Bharat Mein Bandhua Majdur* and edited three sets of stories. Fifteen of her major works have been translated into other Indian languages. Mahasweta Devi also edits the journal *Bartika,* which features contributions from the tribal communities she works with. "Bayen" has been adapted for the stage.

GEETA DHARMARAJAN writes for children and adults. Her works have been published in India and abroad. She served as an editor for *Target* and the *Pennsylvania Gazette,* the alumni magazine of the University of Pennsylvania. She now writes and edits *Tamasha!,* a magazine for first-generation school-goers. She is also the editor of the *Katha Prize Stories,* an annual anthology of the best of Indian regional short fiction in translation. She started Katha in 1988 and is its executive director.

MAMONI RAISOM GOSWAMI, also known as Indira Goswami, is a celebrated name in the field of Asomiya (Assamese) literature. She blends scholarliness with creativity and has a number of novels and short stories to her name. She has received several awards and prizes, including the Sahitya Akademi Award in 1982. Her writing has been extensively translated into other Indian languages and English. She is also a translator and literary critic. Currently she is head of the Department of Modern Indian Languages and Literary Studies at Delhi University.

QURRATULAIN HYDER, a trendsetter in Urdu fiction, began writing at a time when the novel was yet to establish itself as a serious genre in the poetry-oriented world of Urdu literature. She lifted the genre out of its stagnation, and divested it of its obsession with fantasy, romance, and facile realism. She offered it extraordinary range and depth, and brought to its ambit hitherto unexplored terrains of human thought and sensibility. She has several collections of short stories and a number of novels to her credit. Widely traveled, she has also worked in England as a journalist. Many of her books have been translated into Indian and foreign languages. She has received many literary awards, including the Jnanpith Award (1990). She is at present a fellow of the Sahitya Akademi.

VISWAPRIA L. IYENGAR is one of India's younger writers in English. She has been involved with both creative writing and journalism. A deep-rooted concern for social and political problems informs her work. Besides short stories, she has written poetry, plays, and children's books. She is currently working on a film script on child labor.

ANUPAMA NIRANJANA was a medical practitioner by profession until she became a full-time writer. She has published fifty-one books, including novels, short-story collections, travelogues, an autobiography, books for children, and popular medical books. She has received the Karnataka Sahitya Akademi Award and the Sovietland-Nehru Award. She died in 1991.

TEJASWINI NIRANJANA teaches English literature at the University of Hyderabad. She has lectured at universities in the West Indies, Brazil, South Africa, Hong Kong, Taiwan, Japan, the United Kingdom, and the United States. Besides works of literary criticism, she has published two volumes of poetry in English and numerous translations from Kannada into English, including that of M. K. Indira's celebrated novel *Phaniyamma.*

MRINAL PANDE is an award-winning writer, dramatist, and journalist with four collections of short stories, three novels, and five plays to her credit. She is known for her incisive and thought-provoking writings on contemporary women's issues in India. She has been the editor of the popular women's magazine *Vama* and later of *Saptahik Hindustan,* and has received a number of awards for journalism.

URMILA PAWAR is a Marathi writer, many of whose stories are based on the difficulties of living as a woman and as a Dalit. The frank and direct manner of her storytelling has made her a controversial writer in Marathi. She is the author of two collections of short stories, *Sanav Bote* and *Chauthi Bhinta,* which have won many literary awards.

T. JANAKI RANI is a writer known in her mother tongue for writing stories that never deviate from life. Her style is one of powerful understatement. Winner of the Gruhalakshmi Swarna Kankanam Award for writing, she has also received many awards as a producer of radio plays for women and children.

VAKATI PANDURANGA RAO is a writer, translator, and critic. He is the author of more than twenty-five books, and he translates from and into Tamil, Telugu, and English. Currently he is the deputy editor of the *Andhra Prabha Illustrated Weekly.*

JAI RATAN is a well-known translator from Hindi, Punjabi, and Urdu into English. A founding member of the Writer's Workshop, Calcutta, he has edited and translated several collections of short stories.

RUPAVATI—Despite our best efforts we have not been able to locate any information about the author of the story "Thayyaal."

RAJEE SETH has degrees in English and Hindi literature from Lucknow University and has studied comparative religion and Indian philosophy at the Gujarat Vidyapeeth in Ahmedabad. She writes in Hindi and is the author of three collections of short fiction and one novel. Her books have won many awards, including the Rachna Award, the Bharatiya Bhasha Parishad Award, and the Hindi Academy Award. She has also translated the German poet Rilke's letters.

ABOUT GARUTMÄN

Garutmän is an organization that aspires to publish quality Indian literature. It attempts to overcome the main hurdles in transcultural communication in order to project the core of Indian literature while staying as close to the original sources as possible.

Garutmän is a sponsorship body mainly concerned with establishing a community of translators and providing them with required assistance. It organizes translation workshops, processes translations through a panel of editors, and arranges for the publication and distribution of translated works and significant works of Indian literature, both in India and abroad.

Founder Editors
(Late) S. H. Vatsyayan
Vidya Niwas Misra

Board of Advisors
Vidya Niwas Misra
Ratna Lahiri
U. R. Anantha Murthy
A. Ramachandran

Directors
Rekha Mody
Neeru Poddar